The
Chinese
Garden

D1004501

The Chinese Garden

Rosemary Manning

Afterword by Patricia Juliana Smith

THE FEMINIST PRESS
AT THE CITY UNIVERSITY OF NEW YORK

Published by The Feminist Press at The City University of New York
The Graduate Center
365 Fifth Avenue
New York, NY 10016
feministpress.org

First Feminist Press edition, 2000

Originally published by Jonathan Cape, London, 1962

Library of Congress Cataloging-in-Publication Data

Manning, Rosemary.
    The Chinese garden / Rosemary Manning.
      p. cm.
    ISBN 1-55861-215-7 (alk. paper) —ISBN 1-55861-216-5 (pbk. : alk. paper)
      1. Teenage girls—Fiction. 2. Somerset (England)—Fiction. 3. Boarding schools—Fiction. 4. Lesbian teenagers—Fiction. I. Title.
    PR6063.A385 C47 2000
    823'.914—dc21
                                                                        99-056679

This publication is made possible, in part, by public funds from the National Endowment for the Arts and the New York State Council on the Arts, a State Agency. The Feminist Press would also like to thank Florence Howe, Joanne Markell, Jo Ann McGreevy, Caroline Urvater, and Genevieve Vaughan for their generosity in supporting this publication.

Printed on acid-free paper by RR Donnelley & Sons
Manufactured in the United States of America

05 04 03 02 01 00   5 4 3 2 1

FOR ANN

*With much adoe was I corrupted and made to
learn the dirty devices of this world.*
                                    THOMAS TRAHERNE

CHAPTER ONE

<hr>

Surgit, et aetherii spectans
orientia solis lumina.
                              VIRGIL

(He rose and watched the dawning light of the sun in the sky.)

I WAS at boarding school for my sixteenth birthday, for it
falls at the beginning of November. I climbed out of bed
very early that morning, wrapped my dressing-gown round
me and went to the window. The other members of the
dormitory were still sleeping under bright red blankets.
The window, as always in our spartan establishment, was
wide open top and bottom, but I could hardly have been
conscious of the cold air streaming in, for the room was
never filled with anything else and my lungs had been
breathing deeply of it all night. After four years, the code
of Bampfield had fixed its iron bands around my spirit,
and my innate puritanism so welcomed it that I found
a deliberate pleasure in a mortifying regime of cold
water, draughts, outdoor drill and bad food. Although
I now look back on that regime with repugnance, I
can summon up my gratitude for the trained indifference to discomfort and cold which enabled me to sit
almost naked at an open, November window, and watch
the sun rise.

For four years, during most of the weeks of the year, I
had looked out every morning upon the same spectacle,
the great desolate park, low-lying and swampy near the

house, then rising gently towards its farthest boundaries and crowned with a little wood. The rise was only a small one and beyond the park a modest range of hills, some three or four hundred feet high, could be seen lying in a crescent round the head of the vale, of which the park was almost the lowest section. Above the red fields, copses fringed the ridge like curls above a rubicund face. On the highest point of these hills there stood a group of Wellingtonias, planted so closely as to present one statuesque mass. They looked like a brooding figure and were known to us as Moses. They were so much a part of the scene, visible from almost every window of the school, that I can never call to mind the expanse of the park without seeing that lofty, immobile figure on the hill.

> Could we but climb where Moses stood,
> And view the landscape o'er;
> Not Jordan's stream, nor death's cold flood,
> Should fright us from the shore . . .

we used to sing in the school chapel, and staff and children would look at one another and smile, united more surely in that one foolish moment than at any other.

*   *   *

Across the park, dividing the lower marshy flats, with their clumps of rushes, from the mild acclivity which formed the farthest boundary, ran a small stream, with red, crumbling banks. Once it had been spanned at intervals by ornamental bridges, but these were now neglected and ruined and so unsafe as to be almost unusable. At each bridge had been planted and fenced a small shrubbery containing rhododendrons and azaleas. Though these were thickly overgrown they were still bright with colour in spring and early summer, and in winter their foliage made a series of dark pools across the pale yellow-green of the park. The trees were not planted thickly. They stood in small clumps, and they, too, had been long neglected. A surprising number of them seemed to have been struck by lightning. In winter, when their living fellows were leafless, it was hard to distinguish the quick from the dead. Most of these trees were beeches and elms, and their trunks and branches were bleached as white as skeletons. The dead and deformed trunks, standing erect in the frosty landscape, the stiff rime-encrusted rushes, the bare trees, suggested a petrified forest. It was only saved from conveying an air of dreadful corruption and soft decay by its bracing armour of frost. When I became acquainted with the works of the Brueghels, I more than once recognized this same postponement of imminent corruption, as though the hand of winter could only arrest and temporarily conceal a natural and inevitable decay.

Yet though I see this landscape frostbound, it was not a bitter or repellent frigidity which encased it. It was too soft a climate for that. It was arcadian with the gentle, forlorn arcadianism of *The Deserted Village*, which became one of my favourite poems. Its structure was that of a landscape in a classical painting: the clump of trees, the gently rising slope in the background, the river and the road winding from the house to the lodge, leading the eye through the middle distance, and curling out of sight behind the hill. Only the strict orderliness, the neat prosperity of those landscapes was absent.

Describing it now, I remember a melancholy place of

bleaching bones and dilapidated bridges. It did not seem so to me as a child. Then, even in the depths of winter, at its most forlorn, it appeared wholly beautiful. Its ruin was invested not so much with romance or terror as with a pathos which endeared it to me. Perfection I might never have possessed, but this unwanted, neglected park I took to my heart and made my own.

It was my fourth winter at Bampfield and I had seen the cold park dawn-flushed many times before. Moments of experience too often lack some necessary ingredient to render them memorable, or else include some element like a blister or a tiresome companion which spoils their recollection. But here was a scene of extraordinary beauty and a mood of heightened awareness to record it. I could only have felt as I did on my birthday. I had reached the stage in my lover-like relations with Bampfield of regarding the park and grounds as my personal demesne, and looked upon the sunrise as a personal greeting.

O my America my new found land!

I might have quoted Donne if I had read him then, and without any sense of ineptitude at the substitution of a place for a person, for my attitude to Bampfield was very much that of a lover. I felt possessive and was possessed.

As I sat at the window, the greenish sky was slowly suffused with a dark red stain. The lowering grey clouds were incandescent. Words flickered across my frozen mind and took shape as a poem. I dressed, and the sleepers round me stirred, rose and plunged their faces into icy water. Before any of them was fully dressed, I was out of the room, and down in my form-room, where I was supposed to do early prep. My Smith's Latin dictionary beside me, I created a sort of hybrid sonnet in Latin, a poem of fourteen unrhymed hexameters, a flamboyant word-painting inspired by that violent sunrise blazing over the parkland. Did it include the words *flammantia moenia mundi* – 'the flaming ramparts of the world'? The sonnet has vanished long ago, but that Lucretian phrase evokes for me, even today, the thin tongues of flame above a smooth, incisive line of low Somerset hills.

With breakfast, the world returned – the world of noise, ill manners, bad food, evil smells in sour corridors. The sun had disappeared already and left only a faint remembrance of warmth in the wintry sky. The frost had lost its sparkle, and the rushes, as my feet trod over them at break, were limp and soaking. My friends wished me many happy returns. The faithful Bisto (so called from her likeness to the advertisement), who loved me and whose love was a burden, pressed a small package into my hand. It was a handkerchief with an 'R' painfully worked upon its corner. Bisto had no means of washing and ironing it, and it was grey in colour and rather creased. I experienced a growing depression.

As the day wore on, as parcels from home were opened and letters read, a deeper gloom settled upon me. A birthday laid one open to raids upon one's emotions. The family letters, so demanding, so pathetic, were felt as assaults upon my privacy. I pushed them into pockets and wished they had not been written, yet knew I should have been bitterly hurt if I had not received them. And Bisto – it was like Bisto to spend hours working at something secretly for me, and thrust it upon me, the crown of a term's love and endeavour. For her, I thought savagely, this moment is as painful as it is for me. As long as she was still making the handkerchief she could enjoy it, could dream of the moment of giving. Now it is over. I have been ungracious and she is hurt. I wish no one had known it was my birthday, as Margaret does not know. She, at least, has ignored me.

After dinner, there was a period of comparative peace. I sat at my desk in the form-room, where the others round me were reading for the statutory twenty minutes after lunch. I put the finishing touches to the Latin poem I had written before breakfast, and murmured it through to myself under my breath. I felt restored. Moved by a sudden impulse, I left the form-room and went down to Lower V where Miss Burnett was sitting in charge, gnawing a yellow finger-nail and scowling over Latin exercises. At the time of my sixteenth birthday, I was at the height of my enthusiasm for Virgil, and this was reckoned an eccentricity, for no right-minded child liked Latin.

'*Arma virumque cano*,' Miss Burnett had intoned to the little philistines who composed her Latin class. 'Those are the opening words of Virgil's epic, the *Aeneid*. *Arma virumque cano*. Can anyone tell me what they mean?'

'Love me, love my dog,' answered the form wag.

This was my introduction to Virgil, but I survived it. At the age of sixteen most of one's enthusiasms for things are inspired by enthusiasms for people. It would be in order, therefore, if I confessed that I suffered from a *grande passion* for the Latin mistress, but this was not the case. I did not entirely dislike her. In some ways I found her a congenial spirit, for she posed as a rebel and a misfit in a girls' school. But, emotionally, Miss Burnett did not move me at all. My classicism came to me on a pure intellectual stream and saturated my imagination so thoroughly that I have felt the influence of it all my life.

I laid the poem on the desk, on top of Miss Burnett's pile of exercise books. Thus far I felt privileged, as a poet.

'I wrote it this morning,' I said. 'Before breakfast.' I said nothing of my birthday.

Miss Burnett took the wrinkled notebook and smoothed out the pages. Her tobacco-stained fingers trembled, but her blue eyes lost their restlessness and took on an expression of concentrated interest. She read it carefully and slowly.

'That's a wrong quantity,' she pointed out, but it was said as one critical artist to another, not in a spirit of superiority. 'And that – well, I suppose you can use that word, but it's a bit unusual. Got it out of Smith's?'

'Yes.'

'What were the references?'

'There was only one – Statius.'

'I thought it was silver Latin. Used once and you must choose it.'

'Well, I like unusual words.'

'So do I. I share your liking and I like your poem. May I have a copy?'

'All right. I'll do you one today.'

'Isn't it your birthday?'

'Yes, it is,' I said grudgingly. 'How did you know?'

'Oh, I saw your friend Bisto gazing at you like a mooncalf, and wishing you many happy returns. Shall I wish you many happy returns, Rachel Curgenven?'

The tired sardonic eyes surveyed me. The members of

Lower V were no doubt drinking in the conversation, but the actual participants felt themselves alone in a Lucretian and sceptical world.

'Don't bother,' I said. 'I hate birthdays.'

'I respect your feelings,' said Miss Burnett. 'You had better go back to your form-room.'

———◆———

CHAPTER TWO

Fester'd lilies smell far worse than weeds.
SHAKESPEARE

MISS BURNETT was one of the most bizarre creatures who peopled the landscape of Bampfield. She was of it, yet conspicuous upon it, an exotic but quickly festered flower. She was an unhappy woman. This I knew quite well at the time. It was not a later rationalization. Like most children I felt little or no sympathy for others. My attitude was scientific and curious. To us all the world was for discovery. Sympathy is a kind of comment, and we were not given to commenting. That is why, no doubt, we children at Bampfield survived the regime. Our callousness and ignorance insulated us against it, and our scientific curiosity made it bearable. It was the particular world which we were discovering, and we knew no other. In addition, we had, of course, our idealism, an empty vessel waiting to be filled, and soon to be stuffed with the absurd belief that our discomforts were noble and our deprivations sanctified. That the staff, or most of them, accepted the regime so readily, confirms me in the belief that school teachers retain just those features of childhood – its credulity and its uncritical, indiscriminate attitude to the material world – which in a grown-up are least attractive.

At Bampfield the staff was swallowed up by the regime, and found relief, I suppose, from its rigours in administering it with merciless energy to others. It had the virtue of being clear-cut and easily comprehensible. The regime left no one in doubt of its aims, for these were being everlastingly proclaimed, and no member of the staff could be excused on the grounds of ignorance. With the exception of Miss Burnett, they thought it a good regime or persuaded themselves to think it so.

Of the Bampfield figures, Miss Burnett comes first to my mind, because she more than any other epitomizes for me that lovely, sterile decaying Somerset landscape. She was herself – lovely, sterile, decayed. There hung about her, like the aroma of tobacco which she exuded so strongly, an air of corruption. She was so world-weary, so bored with life, so contemptuous. As I recall her, with her golden hair, and her slouching, tired walk, I am irresistibly reminded of Blake's sunflower, weary of time. Yet she was still a very young woman when I knew her, certainly not more than twenty-four or -five. Her spirit was sour and discoloured. She was not wicked, like Miss Christian Lucas. She was irremediably corrupt. She did not bring about this corruption from within herself. She attracted it from without, absorbed it and then exhaled it. Perhaps this was the result of her immersion in the peculiarly saturating atmosphere of Bampfield. Given other circumstances, I believe she would have flowered and given off a pleasanter spiritual aroma. It may appear somewhat of a paradox, then, that she posed as a rebel of the regime, but it was so. She washed her hands of the system, yet she was deeply imbued with it. Her overt contempt for it was expressed in a kind of personal *reductio ad absurdum*. She pushed it to its logical conclusion. She presented in herself the finished product of Bampfield: she flaunted it, she advertised it as if to say – 'Take Bampfield in large doses and become what I am.'

In a school where the feminine was in any case at a discount, where most of the staff wore severely cut suits, and shirts with collars and ties, Miss Burnett, whose looks were utterly feminine, went to extremes and adopted a purely masculine style of dress. She achieved this by a deliberate plan. First, she arrogated to herself the job of looking after the hens. She was not overburdened with teaching, and the Headmistress, Miss Faulkner, who liked ideas and incongruities, was delighted with the bizarre proposal that the classics mistress should take charge of the poultry. The few hens the school possessed were augmented by a large number of new pullets. In the pleasure gardens of the mansion which was our school, were huge, empty aviaries. The hens were put into these, and rooted and scratched amid the exotic shrubs and trees which had once been planted to provide a natural habitat for golden pheasants and other, even stranger, fowl. Miss Burnett's duties with the hens, to which her Latin teaching soon became merely an interruption, allowed her the privilege of wearing breeches, and it was not long before she was wearing them all day. She sported a rather smart suit made of iron-grey heavy linen.

The breeches were very wide, and the jacket was of the Norfolk type, having a stitched belt and pockets with buttoned flaps. In summer she wore green Aertex shirts with dark green ties, and in winter, a green polo-necked jersey.

When she taught, she slipped a gown over her chicken suit, and would sit at her desk, with her tired, sardonic eyes surveying us all as though she hated us, her hands exuding a strong smell of chicken food and Turkish cigarettes (which

17

she smoked incessantly when not actually in the form-room). At the end of a lesson, she would shut her book with a sigh of relief, slip off her gown and toss it to one of us with the curt command, 'Take it to my room.' Then she would slope off in her long, shambling stride, and fumble in her pocket for her cigarette case before she was out of the door.

My ability at Latin awoke in her an old devotion, and she concentrated upon me the narrow but brilliant beam of her intelligence and enthusiasm. She inspired me with a passion for the curiosities of Latin grammar and syntax, so that I was induced to compile a vast book of these eccentricities. I developed a tremendous appetite for middle voices, modal ablatives, and exclamatory infinitives, and my reading of classical authors was considerably enlarged by this pursuit of grammatical curiosities. The passion for collecting is supposed to be very strong in children. My interest in stamps was short-lived, and I never cared for birds' eggs or butterflies, but I would search a volume for a 'Me miserum'!

Looking back on the women who peopled Bampfield, I see Miss Burnett as the one least amenable to the regime, and at the same time, the one most corrupted by it. Those whose spirits were more readily assimilated took their saturation well. No awkward reaction set in. They soaked up the infection and lost their natural colour quickly, like clothes in a vat of dye. It was only Miss Burnett's stubborn spirit which, in resisting the process, set up a fermentation which soured and spoilt her natural fabric. By a vigorous assertion of her personality, Miss Burnett retained a measure of independence, but she retained it only by virtually destroying herself. Real independence would have meant leaving the place altogether and this she could not do. She was rooted in it. Lesser beings were gratified by finding in the regime a framework for their mild eccentricity. Only Miss Burnett knew it for what it was and was compelled to look for her own support. She found it in the cynicism which upheld her like a brace.

CHAPTER THREE

Now the day is over,
Night is drawing nigh,
Shadows of the evening
Steal across the sky.
                    S. BARING-GOULD

IT was the evening of Rachel's birthday. Prep was over, and
the cocoa and slabs of bread, grey and solid, were eaten.
Nothing had been said. It was by a sixth sense that the three
girls knew, as they sat round the form-room fire in silence,
that one of them had withheld something. Incurious, pre-
occupied with their private worlds, they were none the less
sensitive to this unrevealed secret, as they might have been to
a faint and indefinable scent. The fire of logs blazed in their
adolescent, sleepy faces. The stolen chestnuts blackened on
the iron bars of the grate. Occasionally one exploded, and
Bisto would lean forward, lick her fingers, and hook it
expertly out of the hot ashes. She always gave it to Rachel.
If it was refused then she offered it to Margaret. The grate
was small, and they sat round it on hard, wooden chairs,
almost knee to knee. Their black stockings made a paling
through which a few bars of warmth reached the younger
children, who were huddled against their desks in the outer
cold, reading dog-eared novels from the library – novels
which told of midnight feasts, adorable games mistresses and
unbelievable escapades out of school bounds. Within the fiery
circle the three friends, half-stupefied with heat, waited for
the mysterious news that they sensed in their midst. The huge

windows of the form-room were uncurtained. Outside, the winter evening was starless. The cold pressed palpably against the sable glass. Far away in the hollow shell of the building, the eight-thirty bell sounded. It grew nearer, and bored hungry children who had hardly felt the warmth, hurried to the door, glad to go to bed in even colder dormitories. The three by the fire stayed on, ignoring the bell, slowly chewing the last remaining half-cooked chestnuts. The brown skins littered the hearth. The pressure of imminent departure induced Margaret to speak at last.

'I have found something,' she said. 'I've found a strange place that I don't think anyone else knows about. Maybe I'll show it to you tomorrow.'

Almost too hot and exhausted to reply, Rachel stretched her legs lazily towards the powdery ash and without much interest asked, 'What is it?'

But Margaret refused to say more. She glanced at Bisto. 'If I feel like it I'll show it to you, when we can get away from the mob.'

'How can you have found anything today?' asked Rachel suddenly. 'You can't have gone out – it wasn't a games afternoon. It was art. If it's the cellars, Bisto and I found them ages ago.'

'Oh, them!' answered Margaret scornfully. 'Yes, I know them. They smell and are altogether beastly. It's not the cellars. As a matter of fact, I did go out.'

Bisto and Rachel looked at her with admiration. It was no small feat to elude the vigilance of the mistress on duty in the afternoon – or the evening, either, for at this point, the door opened and they were told peremptorily to go to bed. Early to bed and early to rise was the rule of Bampfield. But they would not obey with too great a show of readiness. It

21

was not their policy. Leaving Bisto still raking the ashes for chestnuts, Margaret and Rachel wandered away from the fire to one of the windows. Angrily a hand switched off the light. Looking through the reflections of the fire in the glass, they could see beyond, darker than the darkened sky, the forms of trees, the outline of the distant hill, and the dense mass of a shrubbery.

'Over there,' said Margaret softly, nodding her cropped head. 'Over there.' She looked back over her shoulder for a moment at Bisto. 'I'll show you tomorrow ... perhaps. Depends what I feel like.'

It was part of Margaret's attraction that one never knew where one was with her. In a world of iron routine, in a climate almost invariable, Margaret provided an exotic eccentricity. To begin with, she did not look like a school-girl. She was tall and thin, with a lean, brown, saturnine face, hair cut as short as a boy's, and heavy, often furrowing brows over dark eyes. A passionate reader and an inspired talker, she lived a life balanced between bouts of taciturn isolation, buried in books, and extreme gregariousness, when she attracted to herself those, like Rachel, who found her talk fascinating, and others who found it dangerous or amusing. Together, the previous term, she and Rachel had edited (and largely written) a magazine, in which poetry and parody, virulent comment on the Bampfield regime, and philosophizing on life in general, were welded into a whole by the brilliant editorial hand of Margaret. She was the only spirit among the girls to whom Rachel, blatantly anti-games and fervently intellectual, deferred, for Margaret, totally uninterested in all forms of sport, had forfeited the right to appear on the games field through stubbornly refusing to hit the ball if it reached her. She did this, not because she could not have played games well if she had given her mind to them, but from principle, and this increased the admiration the intellectual set felt for her. Rachel's own case was different. She hated games because she could not play them, and for Rachel it was essential to do a thing well, otherwise it was a torment to her. She did not feel equal to emulating Margaret's ruthless tactics and even – with the ambivalence that characterized her attitude towards Bampfield – made sporadic efforts to achieve something on the games field. But she was never at home with the athletic set, and rendered herself an object of distrust to them by ridiculing them whenever she felt her own inadequacy in their sphere. But in Margaret she recognized one whose chief delight, like her own, lay in intellectual pleasures, and she recognized also, with a certain envy, the consistency of character which she did not herself possess and had begun even then to desire. Rachel mocked incessantly at Bampfield, but secretly she loved it. She would have preferred to loathe it whole-heartedly as did Margaret, who frankly regarded it as a passage through purgatory. Rachel observed towards it a Catullan love-hatred of which she was sometimes ashamed. Once she had found Margaret brooding over a translation of Dante's *Inferno* which she had discovered in the library, with illustrations by Doré. 'Doré might have known Bampfield,' Margaret had remarked bitterly, with that Byronic gloom which Rachel so much admired and to which she was by temperament as well as physiognomy quite unsuited. She held the book open at one of the gruesome delineations of souls in torment. Rachel was merely amused. Her mind ran swiftly to parody. The book was a spur to her restless mind, perpetually seeking new material on which to exercise its growing muscles.

'Let's write a new *Inferno*,' she suggested. '*The Bampfield Inferno.*'

But Margaret at once shut the book secretively and refused to co-operate. Rachel saw her several times that winter, poring over the book in a corner of the library, dwelling with fascinated horror on the pictures of torment, and scanning the text for lines which confirmed her view of Bampfield, while Rachel, at a near-by table, would be translating the *Aeneid* with classical ardour, in the manner of Milton, or scribbling comic verses in the manner of C. S. Calverley. By this time the magazine was dead. Rachel would have continued it, but Margaret sucked the heart out of any enterprise quickly, and refused to embark on a second edition.

Tonight Rachel was too tired to be provoked by Margaret's secretiveness, desiring only to achieve in the setting of Bampfield the equilibrium which her birthday had disturbed. She was almost glad that Margaret had not told them the secret, for she could not have endured any more demands upon herself. In silence, drugged with heat, and the various and incommunicable emotions which weighed upon their hearts, the three left the darkened form-room.

The corridors had long ago absorbed the cold of winter. Wainscot and gilded cornice and bare walls gave off a chill that enveloped them as they went up to bed. In silent files, girls were moving along to their dormitories. No warmth of speech or laughter thawed the icebound surface of the walls. To Bisto it was alarming. Her wrinkled, old-woman-ish face became even more shrivelled. She was acutely sensitive to the spartan discomforts of Bampfield. Her hands and feet were perpetually chilblained, for her mittens were confiscated over and over again as being too hedonistic for Bampfield's stern regime. Her nose was raw with indigestion and her eyes perpetually anxious, on the lookout for some fresh indignity to her unhappy, protesting body.

Margaret whistled defiantly down the silent corridor towards her dormitory. For her, the rules existed only to be broken. She was openly contemptuous of them. A born rebel, she would have been obliged to invent the regime if it had not existed, merely in order to kick against it.

But Rachel, last of the three to go up, paused in the long gallery. She herself slept in one of the rooms opening out of it. It led right across the front of the house and was approached by a fine double flight of stairs, gracefully curving out on either side. On the walls above the staircase hung portraits of the noble family who had once owned the house. And here for a moment, Rachel would stand, if she could find a time when the gallery was empty, as it was tonight. Behind closed doors she could hear the chatter of voices. They might have been the voices of girls dressing to go to a ball. Occasionally, a deeper alto tone brought the illusion of masculine presences, tying cravats, pulling down flowered waistcoats over silk breeches, preparing for the moment when the bells would ring, music play and the stairs fill with figures on their way down to the ballroom. A door opened at the end of the gallery. Amid a cloud of steam, there emerged a ruddy, pyjama'd figure, glistening from her bath. Rachel watched her scurry into a near-by room, her dressing-gown streaming out behind her, then turned away to her own dormitory, Margaret and Bisto forgotten, her birthday shrugged off at last.

None of the three slept in the same room. Their secrets would never be whispered in the dark or behind cover of a

25

curtain, and each adopted, among the girls she slept with, another personality. Bisto was talking to her neighbour in the next cubicle of trivial things, and even giggling a little, tense with suppressed excitement. Unhappy in her relations with the staff, she joined with desperation in the by-play of her fellows, content to be the scapegoat for their lawlessness, if only they would admit her to their sorority. Tonight she hugged herself with secret pleasure, even as she talked. The true world was with Rachel and Margaret, and over the circle hung a mystery. When the lights bell rang, she relapsed easily into silence and let the others whisper without her. Her eyes under their heavy arched brows were wide open. She lay awake with her thoughts, watching the black, shadeless electric bulb swinging in the wind across the square of dark sky.

Up in one of the front dormitories, with their moulded plaster cornices, their tapestry papers, and once polished floors, Rachel was giving a lifelike impersonation of the Head delivering her assembly harangue of that morning. It was a frequent performance, eagerly looked forward to by the rest of her room-mates. The surface mechanism of her mind played a brilliant light over the feeble structure of the morning address and sent underfoot the rags of consciousness that remained from the day's emotions. The room was full of malicious laughter. A bell rang.

'And now to Gud the Father, Gud the Son, and Gud the Holy Ghost,' said Rachel solemnly, and switched out the light.

*   *   *

Down far corridors, voices were talking. Their tones reached Margaret's ears as she lay in bed, her book in its

26

brown paper cover now tucked beneath her pillow. They are talking of me, she said to herself, with bitter conviction. But I shall elude them. Perhaps I shan't ever tell the others of the discovery. They might give it away, and it could have been a secret place for me. No one is to be trusted. Except perhaps Rachel. The voices came a little nearer. She could clearly distinguish them. Matron's voice and Georgie's. She thought contemptuously, they are standing in the passage and talking about me. Georgie is telling Matron that I went out this afternoon, for she did see me, only she didn't dare say anything to stop me. What cowards women are. All except Chief.

From a near-by bed came a whisper: 'Margaret, are you awake?'

She did not answer. *You*, she thought, I will trust least of all.

The speaker called again, a little louder, and a child in another bed stirred in its half sleep.

'Be quiet,' said Margaret in a low voice. 'Be quiet. Not tonight.'

Until she fell asleep, she could hear a stifled sobbing coming from the other's bed.

CHAPTER FOUR

———————

Feed apace then, greedy eyes,
On the wonder you behold:
Take it sudden as it flies,
Though you take it not to hold.
When your eyes have done their part
Thought must lengthen it in the heart.
AUTHOR UNKNOWN

I WAS often restless at night. The vast house, with its silences, folded in mists, an island in a grey, gently moving sea, amid which the black heads of the elms emerged like volcanic islands: the sudden bursts of sound, the opening and shutting of doors, which came to me long after my companions were asleep and brought me back with a jolt to the realization that it was not, in fact, the middle of the night, but only the end of the day for the adults who lived so close to us yet so cut off; the incomprehensible fragments of conversation over-heard on the landings, laughter, or sudden breathing silences when footsteps had stopped near by – all these were part of my experience and a part which bore no relation to the world of day-time. I did not connect the words I heard, the footsteps, the laughter, the silences, with the gowned beings who taught me Latin or History or Games. When night fell, it was as though the building were occupied by a different set of people; I myself changed, and, by being a participant, if only on the fringe of this nocturnal life, I became a different person from the Rachel of my day-time hours. During the day, I worked and played and talked, and lived the limited routine of the school. At night I lay in bed, or sometimes walked about the dark passages unobserved, and my mind absorbed avidly a host of strange and new impressions which were, it seemed, erased by sleep. But it was not so. Gradually I built up a knowledge which I only comprehended years later.

On the night of my birthday I was restless. I slept for a short while and woke to find the room full of moonlight, and that never-forgotten stillness of the night world which made me feel I had awoken somewhere else in space and time. I lay for some while, watching the bar of light shift a little across the beds of the sleepers, and then, fully awake, I got up and put on my dressing-gown. I was cold, as one usually was on winter nights at Bampfield, and went down to my own form-room, hoping that the log fire had retained sufficient embers for me to blow it into life again. Lights were still burning in the hall, and under one or two staff doors. It was half past eleven. The fire was quite dead, but the room was warm, and smelt of ink and wood-smoke. Above me were the rooms of my housemistress, Georgie Murrill. I could hear her walking about. I sat very still by the black grate and ate a half-raw chestnut which was lying in the ashes.

The form-room I was in was next door to the entrance hall, an oasis of Georgian splendour in the midst of inky form-rooms and stone-floored passages. It was a wide hall, with graceful Ionic pillars supporting the gallery above, and it was filled with rugs and fine furniture. It was out of bounds to the girls. Only at night had I ever ventured into it, and there I found a pleasure to my senses, utterly starved at Bampfield, in running my fingers through the thick fur of a

polar bear skin or burying my face in bowls of chrysan-
themums, or other flowers which decorated the carved
chests. The pillars were smooth and cool, and there were
ornaments to handle, and the pictures to look at. I knew it
all well, and gained from it more than the single sensuous
pleasure – a delicious fear of discovery which was exhilar-
ating, and a feeling of private ownership, as though only I
knew this night world of soft lights and shadows. It was a
world of eyes and hands and ears, made the more sensitive
by the necessity to be on the alert to avoid being caught.
Often I identified myself with some personage in one of the
pictures, a knight escaped from battle, in which I saw him
depicted, lance in hand, his horse with staring eyeballs,
straining beneath him. In me, he travelled beyond the
picture and entered some strange, silent hall, and stood alone
as I was standing, sensations washing round him in the
silence, sword in hand against the possible danger. Or the sea
engulfed, at last, the mariner clinging to the spar, and he
entered a drowned world and wandered in caverns lit only
faintly by the reflected light of the sun's rays. And all this,
which seems so endless to me, as though time had no part
in it, all this must have happened within a few minutes, and
on occasions so infrequent that had I ever thought to count
them, they could not have amounted to more than a dozen
in my whole six years at Bampfield.

That night of my birthday, I was interrupted and nearly
caught. I had left the form-room and gone out into the hall
and was lying down on the polar bear rug, revelling in its
soft warmth. Suddenly the windows lit up as a car's lights
travelled quickly towards the house. There was a sound of
brakes. It could only be Miss Faulkner, the Headmistress,
whom we knew as 'Chief'. She alone possessed a car. Doors

opened and shut with quiet solicitude for the sleeping children in the dormitories above, and footsteps crunched over the flints towards the front door. I had no time to get up the long flight of stairs or to retreat again into the form-room. I crouched behind one of the chests and held my breath.

Chief came in, her rubber-soled shoes padding lightly over the stone floor. She was alone. The car drove away again, round to the small garage beside the house. She paced up and down the hall, whistling softly. At last, after what seemed to me an interminable time of waiting, the front door opened again, letting in another blast of cold air, and some-one came in. There was not a sound. The two stood in the hall in silence, but I could not see who the other was. Tense myself, it was only my own tension, perhaps, that abated as the footsteps began to walk towards the stairs, yet it seemed as if some sudden stiffness in the very texture of the air about me slowly relaxed as they moved away from the hall. As they turned the corner of the staircase, half-way up, they came into my view – Chief and Miss Burnett. Chief's arm was round the other's shoulders. A door opened along the corridor above, and Chief's arm dropped. The two stood on the stairs, full in my vision, looking up towards the gallery. Hard-heeled shoes emerging on to it were easily recognizable as Georgie Murrill's. There was a long, weighted silence. Chief turned and looked at Miss Burnett, slowly, very deliberately, replaced her arm round her shoulders and they went on up the stairs, out of sight.

I heard their footsteps go along the gallery to Chief's own suite of rooms at the far end. The double doors – mahogany outside, baize within – opened on easy hinges and shut again with a faint thud.

I was about to creep out and go up myself when I heard a movement above me. Miss Murrill was still standing in the long gallery. I heard her hard shoes tread very slowly back to her room, and when her doors were safely shut I made my way up to my dormitory on bare feet, my slippers in my hand.

CHAPTER FIVE

We've never, no, not for a single day,
pure space before us, such as that which flowers
endlessly open into; always world,
and never nowhere without no....
                                    a child
sometimes gets quietly lost there, to be always
jogged back again.

                              RAINER MARIA RILKE

THE following morning a steady rain fell. The clouds which
had coursed all night through the sky had come to a stand-
still, and sunk down over the low hills in a thick grey quilt.
The children in their ill-lit dormitories dressed to the
monotonous patter of the rain against the windows. Walls
sweated. The building felt like the inside of a well. During
the day there was little opportunity for speaking together,
for the three girls seldom foregathered as a trio except in the
private places they knew of in the grounds, and then usually
at the instigation of Margaret. She would never allow her
friendship to be taken for granted. She did not regard herself as part of a trio at all. Both she and Rachel were independent of each other. They sought each other's company
when they needed it, when they had something vital to tell
each other. But when, as so often happened, the fourteen-
year-old Bisto attached herself to Rachel, Margaret was
more reluctant to join her. If Rachel and Bisto invited her to
come to one of their known meeting-places, they would as
often as not wait in vain. For Bisto this was no hardship. She
far preferred to have Rachel to herself. The fascination

33

which Margaret exerted over both of them was in Bisto's case only a reverence for the personality which commanded Rachel's admiration. Like a dog, she would lick the hand of those who smiled on her mistress, and she was equally quick to snap at those who frowned. Rachel loved her with a half-protective, half-exasperated affection. It was as if she split her surface personality quite readily into two and gave half to each of her two friends. To Bisto went the romantic side, the side which fed upon mystery and upon association, which was firmly rooted in the physical delights of childhood, and most of all in the discovery of secret places. But with Margaret, Rachel felt a different sort of kinship. She was drawn to her because in her company the life of the world beyond school was glimpsed beneath the surface of Bampfield, like hidden streams whose windings are heard but only seldom seen. When Margaret withdrew herself, Rachel felt a sudden stillness, as though out of earshot, and was faintly troubled. It was the life of the adult and the intellectual to which Margaret, precocious and eccentric, beckoned her. Rachel was disturbed at its fascination, yet could not but respond. Thus even Margaret's secrecy, which was the secrecy of the adult, had for Rachel an essential rightness, however painful it could sometimes be.

Shut indoors by the now constant rain, tempers were frayed, friendships strained. Bisto saw with grief the great Rachel amusing her form-mates with her mimicry and indulging in savage jokes against junior staff. Detailed for most of the hated supervisory jobs, and lacking the capacity to inspire respect, these wretched art mistresses and music teachers endured in the chilly, stuffy, overcrowded form-rooms a kind of hell, while the rain beat incessantly outside, and there was no one within earshot to hear the yells, the crash of furniture, and their own feeble cries of 'Girls! Girls! *Please* be quiet!'

If Bisto could have hated anyone she might have hated Rachel at these times. Everything she witnessed revolted her gentle nature, yet the pull of her devotion prevented her from absenting herself or averting her eyes. She watched Rachel; felt compelled to watch and was ashamed that she found a certain delight in this cruel and debasing sport. It was as if Rachel were to acknowledge a taste for cutting up kittens alive, and yet, thought Bisto, as she watched her mincing up the music mistresses, this is not the real Rachel. She is doing it because she is unhappy, because that accursed Margaret sits over there reading and will not speak to her, and has said no more about this secret that she has found.

Eventually, bored with her afternoon's activities, and perhaps a little disgusted with herself, Rachel summoned the faithful Bisto. Together they left the noisy classroom and went down the corridor to the music cells. Damp, ill-smelling little cubby holes, unheated and barely furnished except for a moth-eaten piano and stool, they at least afforded privacy. They found an empty one. The keys of the piano were moist and sticky. Rachel shut the lid down and sat on the stool. She laid her Virgil and notebook on the lid and started to work. She was translating Book VIII of the *Aeneid* into Miltonic blank verse, and Bisto, who was not very much interested in Latin, found the poetic frenzy when it came upon Rachel rather hard to bear. Yet it was of course gratifying to think that one knew a future Milton or Dryden. Usually Bisto sat and knitted or worked slowly and painfully on a teacosy for her mother, on which she was embroidering a peacock. But the swift and secret egress from the form-room had prevented her from getting permission to fetch this. And nothing was to be done at Bampfield without permission. In any case, the cold of the music cell would have numbed her fingers. She sat huddled on the bare boards of the dirty floor and dreamed of what Margaret could possibly have to show them.

Bisto was a romantic. Her imagination led her always into the paths of adventure and action. The secret places were for her, doors to a world where she and those she loved and admired became figures of romantic splendour and stature. Margaret's find – was it a hollow tree? A tree in which they could hide from the others and watch them running past at their inane games of tag and prisoner's base? Or was it something more mysterious and evocative like the stone obelisk they had discovered that unforgettable day last summer?

They had left the open paths in the pleasure gardens, to creep furtively under twisted laurel boughs. In these now overgrown shrubberies, there were to be found little ponds, ornamental, neglected clearings once cultivated, and other sad relics of the garden's splendour from the Georgian days. On this occasion, deep in the midst of a shrubbery, they came across a stone obelisk, lying on its side. Carved on it were the words:

IN MEMORIAM

J. W. B.

SEVASTOPOL

1855

They stood reverently in the presence of this stone. Who was commemorated upon it, only to be forgotten? Some member of the family on whose grounds they stood? There was something exquisitely sad about the fallen stone, set up less than a hundred years before to be a permanent record of the family's loss in the service of their country, and now dragged away and buried deep in the memorial laurels.

Bisto, her mind far away from Virgil, closed her eyes to recall the mystery and wonder of that discovery – for she, of the three, secretly rejoiced in it still, though she pretended that it bored her. Round it she had woven a story of heroism. Brave J. W. B. had not died from a cannonball or grapeshot, but by the knife of an assassin who had crept into the wards of Florence Nightingale's hospital where he lay wounded. J. W. B., tossing in a fever, had heard the stealthy footsteps, seen the white-robed figure (a Moslem fanatic) lurking by the door, his eyes shining in the moonlight, his hand clasping a dagger, waiting for the Lady of the Lamp on her rounds, to plunge his assassin's knife into her heart. Gritting his teeth against the pain, the gallant J. W. B. had crawled from his straw pallet across the mud floor of the ward, leaving behind him a trail of blood from his still open wounds. And just as the faint glow of the lamp could be seen approaching through the open door, he had raised his body with a tremendous effort upon his shattered legs and flung himself upon the assassin, to receive a fatal wound and immortality.

This summer they would act it, thought Bisto, she and Rachel and Margaret, in a clearing in the laurels near the fallen obelisk. Margaret would be the assassin and Rachel of course would be Florence Nightingale, and she herself...no, perhaps Rachel had better be the gallant J. W. B., and she would be Florence Nightingale. It was the least interesting part even if in name it was the most famous.

'I've thought out a wonderful play we can do at that obelisk we found last summer,' she said suddenly. It was

Bisto's failing that she always clung tenaciously to things and pursued them, squeezed out of them the last drop they could give, and went on squeezing when there was really nothing more to extract. Rachel was annoyed.

'You've interrupted a wonderful line,' she said severely.

'I'm sorry,' said Bisto, and relapsed humbly into silence and the Crimea. A few minutes later, Rachel put down her pen. Always uncertain at heart of the value of her creative work, Rachel could not bear to keep it to herself. She must read it or show it to others, seek their support for what she had done, seek even their criticism, for adverse comment had a stimulating effect upon her, stiffening up the sinews of her pride and impelling her to revise, cut and even destroy, in the interests of the perfection that she craved. 'Shall I read you what I've done today?' Rachel asked.

Bisto buried her Nightingale drama and, dumb with cold, settled back against the flaking wall to listen to fifty lines of frigid Miltonic blank verse on the subject of Aeneas' shield. Line after line dropped into the cold air of the cell, and Bisto heard them as an isolated series of sounds which held no meaning for her. Misery invaded her heart. Rachel was too clever for her. Was life always to be this way? A cold empty room, and clever unintelligible words? Was there no warmth anywhere, no friendly hand, no friendship without words?

CHAPTER SIX

Timidi dammae cervique fugaces
nunc interque canes et circum tecta vagantur.
VIRGIL
(*The hinds and the nervous, swift-footed stags wander now among the dogs and around the homesteads.*)

THAT night, as I lay in bed, I watched the clouds piling up over the trees in the park. The moon appeared to be racing across the sky and only with difficulty did I succeed in mooring her above one of the elms in the playing-fields. The air lay heavy over the house. A few drops of rain fell on the sill at my shoulder. In the unnatural light, trees and bushes appeared purple and the grass a vivid yellow. Suddenly a brilliant flash split the sky, lighting up the scared faces of the girls around me, and stabbing me so fiercely in the eyes that I was momentarily blinded. I held my breath, waiting for what I knew would come, and with a sudden hissing, as though the lightning were a white-hot bar of iron thrust into water, the rain came down and peal after peal of thunder rumbled above the black clouds.

I never remember the details of the park being invisible to me at night. It was as if I lived perpetually in the land of the midnight sun. There was not a human sound to be heard, except the breathing of my five or six companions; but there were innumerable animal sounds: the sudden scream of a rabbit, for snares were common all over the park and I must have pulled up and destroyed dozens in my six years at Bampfield; the varied hooting and screeching of the owls which I so often saw gliding across the moonlit park between the clustered, top-heavy elms. But the most characteristic sound was one which I imagine few people hear. It was the pistol crack of antler meeting antler. Then would come the rustle and thud of hoofs, as the stags manoeuvred on the muddy ground for position, and *crack!* it would come again, as they locked their heads in combat. Every night the deer would approach the house. In winter they came right up to the walls, and their hoofs made a light rustling over the loose gravel when they left the grass and crossed the sweep of the drive to find shelter under our windows. We heard them coughing and shuffling and blowing through their nostrils, and then, again the sudden sharp crack of antler on antler. In the morning I would lean out and see the soft brown forms lying under the windows, shining with rime, for all the world like glistening seals upon a beach.

The park, in the fresh light of morning, never ceased to delight me: the abstracted air of tree and bush, the long delicate shadows, the rain-dark rushes. At night, too, I knew it. More than once I climbed out of a lower form-room window and stalked out over the grass, to stand under the elms and look about me. The lights of the staff rooms in the house gave me courage, and allowed me to watch in delicious trepidation the dark forms of the moving deer, to listen to the sound of the stream, always much louder at night, and the creak of branches above my head. A nightjar would whirr in the shrubbery, or an owl brush past me like a moth, and I would climb in and make my perilous way back through the dark corridors, and get into bed with my heart beating fast and my mind full of sensations which I have never forgotten.

I came to love my surroundings so deeply that I became a

slave to them. For a few years after I had left school I felt compelled at intervals to return there, not to see anyone, but to renew my relationship with the place, with the shrubberies deep in the leaves of many seasons, the statuesque elms, the derelict park. It possessed me, though I had the illusion of possessing it. I can remember having this strong feeling of possession quite consciously; of saying to myself, as I stood alone on the grass: I belong here. This is my place. This is where my roots are.

While I was at school I never confided this feeling to anyone. I confided it only to Bampfield itself, to the long lime avenues, with their carpet of moss and primroses, to the dark, arcanian shrubberies, and the network of acrid-smelling paths that interlaced them. But when I was with my fellows, Bampfield was to me as it was to them, school. The park was the domain where we strolled on the innumerable occasions when we evaded games; the lime avenues, like the groves of Academe, were fruitful of talk, of endless critical talk. Like lords we walked these tall avenues. I never remember playing in them any of our usual games. They did not lend themselves to frivolity. But there among my confederates I tore the regime to pieces; ridiculed Chief's latest sermon; poured scorn on the prefects who were too scared of us to curb our irredeemably bad behaviour. In the cold, deserted shrubberies, talk became more philosophical. Here we smoked, walking slowly among the laurels and rhododendrons, our feet making no noise on the brown leafy paths, where the leaves of a dozen seasons lay unswept.

And Bampfield gave me my private worlds. I knew many places that hardly anyone else knew. Girls are not adventurous nor are they explorers like boys and few of us strayed from the paths in the gardens or penetrated the overgrown shrubberies along the stream. Nor was I any more adventurous than the rest, but a habit of solitude due to a year of lameness, and the overwhelming desire to know intimately the whole of my domain, led me to explore it inch by inch, though a natural fear of the unknown led me sometimes to take companions with me on my more daring explorations. I found that they seldom wanted to return to these secret places, often difficult of access. I returned alone.

Deep in the shrubberies was a derelict rose garden, well known to most of us as a playground, but only I knew of the little iris garden that lay beyond it, hidden in the laurels, the path to it now completely overgrown. I found it one afternoon in early summer – a small circular clearing in the bushes, carpeted with thick green moss that sank beneath my feet. In the centre were a few neglected shrubs. One was a magnificent fire-bush. Later, on an autumn afternoon I found it blazing in the shadows, untouched by sunlight. All around the long, derelict garden were clumps of iris which, though choked and half-buried in bramble and couch grass, still produced a few flags of brilliant blue and yellow. That was how I first saw it – a little theatre of green desolation, lit with tapers of blue and yellow flame. Later, when high summer came, I used to go there by myself and sit on the dry moss and read Shelley's *Adonais* and Keats's *Hyperion*. The garden was surrounded not only by rhododendron and laurel, but also by tall trees, and looking upwards one would see the sky as nothing more than a small blue plate amid the dense, surrounding green.

For what world was I searching on these occasions, when the urge came upon me to hide even from my closest friends? I did not know. I was aware only of a private delight in and need for the secret places, a delight which

42

was different from the child's pleasure in secrets, and a need greater than the mere desire to escape from school. Bampfield so satisfied a part of my personality that I had no desire to escape from it. But there resided within me, the schoolgirl Rachel Curgenven, another self, a restless, hungry, immaculate being, bent on piercing through the outward semblances of things to seek out another intuitively-known reality, a reality beyond the world as I saw it. Without being aware of it at the time, I brought back, perhaps, no more than the word 'fire' or the word 'rose'. But these images flowered for me in the deserted gardens of Bampfield, and they never withered.

Poetry was the bridge over which I walked to this world which, at sixteen, I was already in danger of losing sight of.

> Names, deeds, grey legends, dire events, rebellions,
> Majesties, sovran cities, agonies,
> Creations and destroyings.

I became intoxicated with the power of poetry to transport me into this other world and resentful of sharing the peaceful places. Only when I was alone could I experience the 'shades and silences and the voices of inanimate things'. They acquired for me a quality of near-perfection, owing to their withdrawn, uncontaminated peace. The lines of their formal beauty remained, the paths could be traced, the urn still stood on its crumbling base, the dry fountain could be seen above the rushes. The image in the eye of whoever had created it still lay behind its dereliction, could be recaptured by my own imagination. It was at the time of my sixteenth birthday that I first became conscious of the power of such images over my being. The sunrise on the November morning remained more vividly in my own mind than in the words in which I had tried to re-create it and share it with others. When I thought of Margaret's still untold secret, I realized that she might have regretted the impulse that made her begin to tell us of it, and I recognized that she had the right to keep it to herself, to preserve it inviolate. Some bond of sympathy between myself and Margaret reduced my curiosity to manageable proportions.

Lying in bed, the morning after the storm, watching the rain, I was almost glad that it would probably be impossible for her to reveal the secret today.

———————

CHAPTER SEVEN

This was my shaping season.
HENRY VAUGHAN

DAY after day it rained with West Country persistence. Rachel threw herself resolutely into her Virgil translation, finished it at last and gave it to Miss Burnett. Bampfield was sodden and inert. Chief had not appeared for days. It was given out that she was ill, and the withdrawal of her presence took the salt out of the regime. At last, the rain cleared and a faint watery sun hung luminous in the sky, giving little warmth but cheering to the eye. Tempers grew easier. No longer confined to form-rooms, the girls ran about the muddy park; windows were opened, and the building began to breathe freely again. Chief recovered. Rachel saw her coming slowly down the front staircase one morning and at once went to her assistance. It was the recognized thing that you offered Chief your shoulder to lean on, coming down stairs. At the bottom, Chief did not relinquish her hold.

'What are you supposed to be doing, Curgenven?' she asked.

We were almost invariably called by our surnames at Bampfield.

'Drill, Chief, I was just going down to change my shoes.'

'Ah, yes, drill,' said Chief, as though hearing of the subject for the first time. 'Never mind, I want to talk to you. Come out into the sun.'

The two walked slowly out, and across the front sweep on to the sodden grass.

'Isn't it awfully wet for you?' asked Rachel protectively.

The habit of protection was well developed in the older girls.

Chief ignored her remark, and leaning heavily on her shoulder gazed at the distant hills.

'That's a very good piece of work you've done for Miss Burnett,' she said slowly. 'Very good indeed.'

For a moment Rachel did not understand her. 'My...my last prose, do you mean, Chief?'

Chief shook her shoulder playfully. 'No, no,' she said. 'Your translation.'

'Good lord, has Miss Burnett shown it to you?'

'Certainly. I read it through last night. I couldn't put it down until I'd finished it. I'm very glad you did it. It is things like that that make teaching worth while.'

Behind them on the cruel flints, the rest of Rachel's form was having drill, making teaching worth while for Miss Christian Lucas. Chief and Rachel walked slowly up and down the hockey pitch, Rachel silent, Chief meditative, speaking from time to time at random, about Virgil, about the pitch, about the prospect of the park.

On this damp November morning, the voice of Miss Christian Lucas, absorbed by the spongy atmosphere, receded as Chief and Rachel went further down the pitch. Half-hypnotized, Rachel suspended both her hatred of Miss Lucas and her morbid passion for the drill itself, and allowed herself to be wholly subject to Chief's personality. She had suddenly started a new subject.

'You will have to be a prefect soon. How do you feel about it?'

No false modesty was expected. Chief uttered the words as a challenge. True to her Bampfield training, Rachel replied, 'I'm ready when you choose to make me one, Chief.'

'Really? Are you ready?' Chief looked at her shrewdly. 'You have still some way to go, I think, but it is something that you feel yourself ready, for that means that you are prepared to train yourself further. Is that so?'

'What do you want me to do, Chief?'

'You must regard yourself as a squire, training to be a knight. The positive qualities I think you possess – a sense of leadership, an air of authority. But there are things you will have to do without. You must remember how an acolyte, before taking his vows, fasted. You will have to learn to fast. Must I tell you what you will have to do without?'

No, it was not necessary. Rachel felt she already knew. Her friendship with Bisto, possibly. Her friendship with Margaret, certainly. A prefect was understood to embrace a vow of non-friendship, much as a knight espoused lady chastity. It was a Bampfield rule.

The two turned and walked back in silence. The voice of Miss Lucas became more insistent.

'*Knees outward...bend!*'

The flints grated beneath twenty pairs of ravined plimsolls. Chief paused. The girls were now running, marching and counter-marching, their breaths coming in uneasy gasps.

'She trains their bodies,' said Chief with admiration, watching the precision of the ranks. 'Only *you* can train your mind, your own personality. With of course, the help of Gud. It is a matter of the will. Train your will first, Curgenven, and all else shall be added unto you.' She leaned a little

47

more heavily on Rachel's shoulder. 'Next year I shall make you a prefect.'

Chief released her, and walked back into the house alone, leaving Rachel standing on the empty hockey pitch, moved and appalled, like a neophyte who has attended some fascinating but revolting rite.

In the park among the decaying branches and ashen trunks of the dead sycamores and elms stood a few young trees, planted before the school took over the estate, and left uncared-for ever since. Each had been given protection from the deer and the rabbits by a circlet of iron paling, to which netting was fastened. The netting had long since rusted into shreds, but the palings remained, close now to the bark they had once protected, and doomed, as the trunks swelled, to throttle the trees more and more tightly, till, like the iron bands of a medieval engine of torture, they cut into the living bark. I see now a symbolism in the deeply scarred trunks. All the ambivalence of my attitude to Bampfield is summed up in that short conversation with Chief as we strolled the playing fields. I despised the regime, laughed at it, rebelled against it, yet I was subject to its fascination. I could not detach myself from it and readily rendered up my personality to its peculiar power. It could not restrain my growth, but, like the iron bands encircling the trees, it could and did mark me.

———————

CHAPTER EIGHT

To submit myself to all my governors, teachers,
spiritual pastors and masters ...
THE CATECHISM

THE school which framed our youth was founded in about
1919 by a group of friends who had met and worked
together in V.A.D. hospitals during the Great War. The
Caesar of this triumvirate was Delia Faulkner. The Lepidus,
who provided the money for the venture, was a Mrs Watson,
a widow with a small girl. The Pompey – though here the
comparison is less apt – was Miss Gerrard, a brilliant
organizer and campaigner in the field of education. Later,
a fourth and much younger woman, Miss Murrill, had been
added to the group.

Miss Faulkner was always called Chief. Not *the* Chief,
but simply Chief.... 'Yes, Chief, no, Chief.'

The school was an amalgam of Sparta, Rugby and
Cheltenham Ladies' College. The first dictated the details of
our physical life, the drilling in wind and rain, the cold
washing water, the bad food, the inadequate heating and
bedding, the hateful runs before breakfast. The third,
Cheltenham, contributed the moral tone of the school, but
the second influence, that of a boys' public school, was in
some respects the most far-reaching, for it governed our
social relations with each other and with the staff.

This Bampfield ideal was designed to turn us into English
gentlemen, *sans peur et sans reproche*. In justice to boys'

49

schools, it must be confessed that the discipline savoured more often of a prison camp than of Eton or Rugby. We marched everywhere in line and in step – to meals, to prayers, to bed. Silence must be observed in every passage, and during part of every meal. No personal possessions were allowed except clothes and similar necessaries. A photograph or a trinket was confiscated at once, if found. We wore a severe uniform which never varied, winter and summer, and which, without being actually masculine in style, succeeded in reducing our femininity to unnoticeable proportions.

Though Chief could not alter the physical appearance of the children completely, she did alter her own. She wore her hair severely cropped like a man's. Her face was of a masculine cast, the nose slightly aquiline, the forehead smooth and high, the chin firm and finely moulded – a remarkable face. Summer and winter, she invariably wore a silk shirt, with detachable soft collar, and a silk tie, under suits which were made for her, of good grey suiting, and cut in as masculine a style as they could be without the actual substitution of trousers for a skirt. When she went out, she wore a green pork-pie hat, and a heavy camel's-hair coat, which I believe was actually bought in a men's shop.

She was not tall, and inclined a little to fat when I knew her, but she was very finely made. Her bones were small and delicate. Her hands, in particular, were of great beauty and she used them expressively. Her mouth could express an extraordinary sweetness, but it was marred by her teeth, which were brown and irregular. Her eyes were a light colour, a kind of greyish hazel. In the old photograph I have of her, and often as I remember her in real life, they had an infinitely sad and haunted look. The spark of her will usually flashed from them, and so dominant and piercing were they that they almost hypnotized one. But in repose, and under the revealing eye of the camera, the scared, unhappy woman that existed in that elegant, tailored dummy, stood out as clearly as ancient earthworks under the turf are revealed by an aerial photograph. A world of mystery lay behind those extraordinary eyes. I used to long to know more about her, but I never discovered very much. According to her own account, she came of an old East Anglian family: she had gone on the stage; she had left it for reasons of health; she was an M.A. of Leeds University (this I never, even at school, believed. I was persuaded that she had selected this university as her Alma Mater partly for its remoteness and partly for the beautiful colour of its Master of Arts hood – a rich blue – which she always wore on Sundays); she had been a V.A.D., and the Matron of a war hospital; and after the war she came to Bampfield to educate girls in accordance with her peculiar principles, certainly no typical schoolmarm, but no normal woman either.

Seated behind her desk, the cropped head above the dark, well-cut suit, the immaculate collar and tie with its unostentatious pin, she gave one the impression of ineluctable masculinity. Parents seemed to find this unexceptionable, and accepted with equanimity the statement that their daughters were to be brought up as public school boys. I can only regard this as a twentieth century refinement of the primitive habit of exposing girl children to perish in earthenware jars.

Chief suffered from what is vaguely termed a weak heart. In 1918, doctors had told her that she was unlikely to live longer than a year. She was then in her early or mid-thirties. She lived, in fact, to be over sixty. And so extraordinarily potent was the spell that she cast over all who knew her, that when I heard of her death, even though I had not seen her for years, and had come to understand Bampfield for what it was, it moved me profoundly, and for days I could think of little else. It was then that there came into my mind an occasion – rather dim to me – which I had not recalled in all the years since I left the school. It hangs now ineffaceably upon the walls of my mind like one of those Netherlandish pictures of the seventeenth century in which a little scene – a figure poring over a manuscript, or a shepherd looking down at the Child in the manger – glows out from a small patch of light amid a surrounding expanse of black canvas. So I see Chief lying on a couch one winter's night, and the couch was not in her study, but up on the wide first-floor gallery. We were coming up the staircase which divided and ascended to either end of the gallery. The hall lights were out and the corridor itself in darkness. Only the little group round the couch was clearly illuminated. And Chief was dying, it was whispered. One by one we came up to the couch and in hushed tones said good-night to her. We had been told that it was her wish to lie there and see us as we went to bed, to hear our voices bidding her good-night for the last time. She herself did not speak. She recovered, and the incident was never referred to again.

She willed herself to live. The will for her was the most important attribute of human nature. Her creed was not so much 'Nothing is impossible to him who believes', as 'Nothing is impossible to him who uses his will-power.' Having proved to herself the undeniable advantages of willing herself alive, she was eager to pass on these benefits to others. Self-control was the watchword of Bampfield, and I am inclined to think there was a fundamental confusion in Chief's mind between the active principle, the will, and the passive virtue of silent endurance. She herself undoubtedly possessed exceptional power of will which enabled her to endure pain and sudden helplessness without complaint, and also perform, and even more often force others, against all odds and opposition, to carry out work she wanted done. I admired her then and I admire her now for that immense, indomitable will-power which kept not merely material difficulties and physical weakness at arm's length, but compelled even Death himself to wait outside the door till she was ready for him. But for children there were no such high stakes. Death and worldly disaster were remote from us, and provided no noble exercise for our powers, which in any case would hardly have been equal to a combat with such majestic antagonists. No, it was our task to strengthen and train our wills in the limited field of school reverses and discomforts, that we might face and overcome the struggles of adult life, the world, the flesh and the devil. To this end generous opportunities for self-denial and endurance were provided at Bampfield.

None of us ever complained. Indeed, why should we? We were told by Chief over and over again that it was 'our' school, and we really believed it. The discomforts seemed perfectly legitimate, like bunkers on a golf course. At any rate, I know I came to regard them in very much that light, as a test of skill and endurance. I learned to accommodate my person to the lumps in the flock mattress and my stomach to the bread and margarine which was our staple diet, while my spirit was fortified by the noble words of Galsworthy which I heard at least a dozen times every term, for it was one of Chief's favourite poems (I hope I remember it correctly):

If on a Spring night I went by
And God was standing there,
What is the prayer that I would cry
To Him? This is the prayer:
O God of Courage grave,
O Master of this night of Spring!
Make firm in me a heart too brave
To ask Thee anything.

We must have felt that not only God, but Chief, was standing there, and a very palpable presence at that. Whatever secret petitions we might in our inner weakness have directed heavenwards, we certainly would have been ashamed to proclaim our cowardice by asking Chief for any remission of our hardships.

Dictator though Chief was, the other two members of the triumvirate which fenced us from the world were more than mere lackeys. Each of them possessed a character of iron, which, joined by the rigid band of a common and apparently uncriticized ideal, dictated the shape of our youth.

The School was called Bampfield Girls' College. I think Miss Faulkner would have liked to call it Bampfield Ladies' College, since Cheltenham was one of her working models, but she hesitated at the plagiarism, and later even the 'Girls' was dropped. The reason for this was, I believe, that she had come by this time to regard us all as boys and did not wish to be reminded of the biological facts.

To Miss Murrill and to the members of the triumvirate, Chief was known as Dick, a tribute, I presume, to her masculinity. The second member of this trio, Mrs Watson, despite the evidence of a daughter, might also have been taken for a man, except that her rotund figure precluded all possibility of her wearing trousers. She, like Chief, wore her hair cropped, but her masculinity had nothing of sex about it. She was a grand old woman and a ripe eccentric. Her humour was, for a girls' school, somewhat Rabelaisian, her temper execrable, and her language of doubtful propriety, but there was about her an inalienable air of good breeding. She came of an ancient and cultured family, and showed it, despite the cropped hair, the sagging tweed skirts and the grubby habits (her room smelt abominably). She was known to her intimates as Punch, and the name fitted her exactly.

Her loyalty to Chief was incorruptible. Her keen intelligence and sceptical, inquiring mind could have made her critical, and I knew, later on, that she never hesitated to argue with Chief, or present to her plainly her own views on a situation, but publicly she gave not the slightest indication that even the most monstrous pronouncements, the most impracticable suggestions, on Chief's part, were alien to her own way of thinking, and she supported them not merely with good humour but with a personal bias which seemed to proclaim them reasonable. I have never discovered the springhead of this devotion. Punch was condemned to discomfort, for she lived in one of the most disagreeable, though picturesque, corners of the house; she drew no salary and had devoted a substantial portion of her capital to the school; and her work was a mere dismal round of teaching in a school where the standard of scholarship was low, and book-learning played a subordinate part to character forming. Scripture must be taught, and Geography must appear on the time-table. Punch took both, doling out to us the needful portions of each, much as though it were a matter of brimstone and treacle. She was only diverted – and diverting – when drawn into the bypaths of knowledge.

It became a matter of tactics to trail red herrings across her path, and she relished the game hugely, casting aside with relief the annotated edition of Genesis, or the out-of-date atlas, and embarking on a detailed explanation of the eugenics of the ring-straked and spotted cattle, or the supposed location of the land of the anthropophagi whose heads do grow beneath their shoulders.

Punch's rooms were at the top of the house in the Tudor wing of the building, and approached either by the old turret staircase, or from the passages which ran right round the top of the school. Off these passages lay twenty or twenty-five rooms, mostly very small. Some of them were allotted to the junior staff, two or three to the prefects for studies, while the larger ones were used as dormitories. They were bitterly cold in winter and insufferably hot in summer, but they had a magnificent view, and outside them was a stone parapet which was the delight of daring spirits. Punch was too indolent and too absorbed in her books to pay much attention to the children in these dormitories, technically under her care and in her 'house'. They were notoriously ill-behaved, and the lives of the prefects whose studies were near by were made a misery by their lawlessness.

Punch's rooms were themselves of unbelievable squalor. In front of the small rusty grate lay a black and red rag hearth-rug, thick with crumbs and hair and coal-dust. In my early days, a dog repellent with age, rheumy of eye and for the most part hairless, lived on this mat. Later he was replaced by a corpulent dachshund whom Punch took everywhere with her at the end of a lead at least ten feet long, fixed to her waistband. With this creature she could be seen from afar off in park and pleasure gardens, a vast rolling barrel of a woman, with a small, fourlegged bottle-shaped dog panting along at a distance of ten feet, the two joined by what appeared to be an umbilical cord.

On the far side of her rooms were the domestic quarters, which ran along one side of the house and were sealed off from the studies and upper dormitories by a locked door. Men and maid servants slept in these tiny attic rooms, an arrangement which the presence of Punch was supposed to regularize. Once, I saw the rooms, I have no idea why. Perhaps it was after the end of term when I had stayed on for a few days. I remember I walked the length of that corridor from the prefects' studies to Punch's quarters. Below me were the noble wrought-iron gates of Chief's private garden, the green turf, the flower-beds a blaze of colour, and the dark yew hedges bordering its brightness. I turned from these windows to look into the rooms, for the doors were open, and I was so sickened that I could hardly refrain from running down that corridor. In those little airless garrets was the most piggish squalor I had ever seen. Beds were unmade, chamber-pots unemptied, chests of drawers lurched sideways, lacking a leg, or hung half open to reveal a few discoloured clothes, and there emanated from those wretched cells, and from the unspeakable lavatory, a smell I shall never forget. Who knew of it? No one. Not even Punch, living within a few yards of that smell, thought it worth while to make those rooms more habitable.

The servants at Bampfield frightened me. They were brutish, but I did not at the time draw the necessary conclusions from what I saw that afternoon. I was only the more disgusted and fearful. One of the servants was an old woman called Bessie who was often to be found lurking in dark corners of the back stairs, and who was, I think, a natural. She spoke an unintelligible Somerset, in which the elisions 'ch'ill' and 'ch'ave' were common and almost the only distinguishable features of her barbaric speech. The servants were no one's responsibility. Their squalor was part of the corruption which festered underneath the smooth Palladian skin of Bampfield. It was one of the many contradictions of the place that Punch, who certainly must have known of that evil corridor, remained indifferent to it, and to the sordid discomforts of her own rooms, and yet displayed in her own person, despite the shabby evidence of her clothes, a fastidiousness, and in her bearing a quality which fitted with absolute harmony into the cultivated home she shared with her sister. I never knew her well enough to find the solution to this contradiction. I leave her in the picture as I saw her for six years, keen-eyed, weather-beaten, good-humoured yet irascible, with a face like one of Rembrandt's women, as wrinkled as a stored apple.

Miss Gerrard, the third member of the triumvirate, was a tall, severe, fine-looking woman, a 'handsome' woman, with blue eyes of the most piercing quality I have ever seen. Her hair was a golden-brown, rather stiff – almost *en brosse* – but at least it was not an Eton crop, and indeed she was not masculine. But neither was she truly feminine. She looked a woman, but somehow every ounce of femininity had been drained out of her and left her a splendid shell, animated by a fierce devotion to work and duty. I never knew her well. Some children were fond of her, but most of us feared her too much for affection. She left when I was about fourteen, and I never saw her again. I have often wondered why she went, and suspect (with no grounds whatever) that there was in her adamant nature a righteousness and high principle which could not in the end countenance the regime for which she was expected to work. We called her the Rock, and she was one of the very few women at Bampfield for whom I felt and still feel an honest respect.

When Miss Gerrard left, her place in the triumvirate was taken by Miss Murrill. She was mildly attractive, with curly hair and a small neat figure. She was lively, and, when in good humour, very charming. When I arrived at Bampfield she was not more than twenty-seven and engaged at the time in a fervent love affair with a local man, of which she later told me some most unsuitable details. Even after her affair came to nothing, she made some effort to retain her femininity. She never got as far as make-up, but she sometimes wore frocks. In keeping with the masculine principle of the place, Chief had christened her Georgie, her Christian name being Georgina.

Mrs Watson, Miss Gerrard and Miss Murrill were housemistresses. I knew only one of them, therefore, at all well, my contact with the other two being limited to the classroom. Though we all lived under one roof, different parts of the building were sacred to different houses; there were house colours and house mascots, and separate dining-rooms. The combined influence of the triumvirate was weaker, therefore, because it was diffused. It reached us in small draughts, in the history lesson, or the house match. Chief's influence, however, reached us wherever we were. Though she seldom met us in the classroom, dormitory or games field, she was present in those places where we were most vulnerable – the chapel and big hall – and she wandered the passages ceaselessly, so that we were always aware of her physical presence. She was not spying on us. It would be unfair to suggest this. She had a beautiful and melodious whistle and this she used as she walked the corridors, to warn us of her coming. She once told me that she had deliberately cultivated the art of whistling for this purpose. Because of this, I do not think I ever feared her as a remote, God-of-vengeance figure. I *did* fear her, but my fear was something far more subtle. I feared the idea of headship, the immanent power of which she was a manifestation. With her actual presence I was often on the best of terms. Yet I knew always that no matter how good-humouredly she fell in with my wildest schemes, no matter how flattering her warm interest in anything I wrote, I was subject to her pervasive will, by a process I was half-conscious of, yet incapable of rebelling against, for a part of my nature enjoyed and was gratified by it. If I am honest, I must admit that many children passed through Bampfield unscathed. If I was one of those who suffered, then it was, at least partly, my own fault, in that there was much that nourished the less creditable sides of my nature, and which I imbibed willingly.

The key figure to this aspect of my youth was Georgie Murrill. There was never a more untrue cliché than that which says we needs must love the highest when we see it. Not only did I like and enjoy the wrong things. I liked, and even loved, the wrong people. For Miss Burnett, to whom I owe so much of what has made life worth living, I felt no personal affection at all. I place on record now a belated tribute to her and to all she gave my adolescent mind. It does not matter to me that she was a failure personally. As far as I am concerned, she was a success, and in trying to discover the sources of my imaginative life, and the roots from which grew my mature self, I am inevitably led to Miss Burnett. Chief was less an influence than an atmosphere in which I breathed. It had certain virtues. It made me resistant to some things, but more prone to others, but I dare say this would have happened wherever I had been educated. My mind and heart were driven to find their nourishment in books and in my evocative and strange surroundings, by the rigid discipline of the school and the physical hardships imposed on us, and by the stifling atmosphere with which Chief surrounded us. I think I was fortunate that Bampfield gave me so much, even if in this negative manner. It furnished me, all unknowing, with a weapon which I was later able to turn against the worst elements it had encouraged in me. At another school I might have been 'made to pattern' and remained so, with no rebel vision to tear away the falsity. Other schools might have had no Chief, and no Miss Burnett. They would, I fear, have had plenty of Georgie Murrills. One was enough.

This young housemistress was addicted to mascots, hockey matches, nineteenth-century history and early Beethoven. It is difficult to resist the charm of such things when one is young, and many people, who have had too many Georgie Murrills in their lives, never grow out of such addictions. To all of them she succeeded in enlisting my devotion, with the exception of the hockey matches. I have nothing against the other three enthusiasms, but they can hardly be said to lead one on to maturity.

She also succeeded in enlisting my personal devotion, as no one else did at Bampfield, and this was an entirely limiting and wasteful experience. It is not possible for an adult to attempt to pull a child into her own adult world, and this is what Georgie Murrill attempted. She treated me as a confederate, elevated me to the position of a confidante and personal assistant in matters relating to the house of which I was later to be captain. She was incapable of seeing me as a child and a rather immature one. She played upon the arrogant side of my nature, allowing me to believe myself a far more grown-up and privileged person than I actually was. Put, as I thought, upon an equality with her, I took the same liberties, and made the same demands which I should have made of my contemporaries. It was unfortunate that I had no contemporaries for whom I cared anything. Bisto was soon to leave and Margaret was inaccessible. I learned to despise my fellow prefects when I became one–blown up by Georgie with self-esteem, and set apart from them in any case by my university work.

Chief, whatever her faults may have been, did not make the mistake of favouring me above my fellows. She encouraged and praised my writing, but she judged my character ruthlessly. She told me bluntly, when she had seen how I behaved as a prefect, that she would never make me head of the school, and she told me why. 'You have not learned to suffer fools gladly,' she said. 'Moreover, you are not reliable enough to be in such a position. Plainly, I do not trust you, completely.'

I was hurt, but she was right. Georgie Murrill, instead of supporting Chief in her verdict, undermined it, allowing me to recover with her the worthless and inflated self-esteem which Chief had refused me. I wish to be just to Chief, aware that I have ridiculed and criticized her. But I find it hard to be just to Georgie Murrill who took so much and gave so little, who sucked the life out of her favourites, but was herself too small and limited a personality to make such an operation in the least worth while to her victims. It is a truism that out of our most wretched and humiliating experiences there is usually something to be gained. I think Daniel might agree that the walk through the fiery furnace was worth the meeting with the three holy children. I am not going to shed tears because I spent my schooldays in a place where many of the staff were morally corrupt, the physical standards those of Dartmoor, the religion perverted and the games mistress a sadist. It looks a formidable list, but children will always be subjected to something. I was not beaten, as I had been at my previous school, by a gang of bullies. I was not underfed. I was not entirely ill-educated. But I find it necessary to place on record that Georgie Murrill, the least valuable in personality, the most trivial in mind, procured my affection and exploited it for her own ends. The full measure of her turpitude will be seen later, when her cowardly desire to appear on the side of the angels led her to jettison the child she should have protected. I think it is for the Georgie Murrills of this world that the millstones are reserved.

CHAPTER NINE

'Boy!' I remember Bowyer saying to me once
when I was crying the first day after my return
after the holidays – 'Boy! the school is your father!
Boy! the school is your mother! Boy! the school
is your brother! the school is your sister!
the school is your first cousin, and your second cousin,
and all the rest of your relations! Let's have
no more crying...'

CHARLES LAMB

IT became colder towards the end of November. The skies cleared. Music and art mistresses licked their wounds and prayed that the fine weather would continue to the end of term. Strolling down to the deserted stables, one afternoon, to see if they could find their pet rat, Bisto and Rachel suddenly stopped in their tracks. They had seen a figure running along by the fence of the big shrubbery on the far side of the stream. It was Margaret. Half-way along the palings, she halted and took something from her pocket. For a few moments she stood there and seemed to be pulling and twisting the wire. 'Right against the forest fence, by St Agnes' fountain,' murmured Rachel, whose mind ran all too easily to facetiae. 'So that's where it is – whatever she found and told us about that night.'

Margaret had undone the wire and was pulling out a paling. She laid it on the ground, squatted down and squeezed herself through the opening in the fence, to disappear in the thick undergrowth inside.

'Shall we follow her?' asked Bisto, in an unnecessary whisper.

'I don't know,' answered Rachel. 'Perhaps we ought not to go at all. After all, it's her secret, whatever it is she's found.'

'She promised to show it to us ages ago,' said Bisto impatiently, 'and she never has.'

'She's probably changed her mind.'

'Then let's follow her.'

'I'd rather wait and see if she tells us,' said Rachel, stubbornly. 'If we go now we might meet her and she'd think we were spying on her.'

'All right,' agreed Bisto, good-humouredly. 'Let's see if Willy's there.'

Willy was our favourite rat. We fed him on pieces of school dinner which he liked far better than we did, and he grew quite tame. We had met him at the very beginning of the term and visited him at least once a week.

The stables lay at the end of an overgrown carriage-way, almost half a mile from the house. The silent bell still hung in the turret and beneath it the stable clock, with its stained, immobile face. This had lost its hands long before, and its timeless dial gazed fatuously up the decrepit lime avenue. The stable gates were rotting and half open. Inside, grass was growing over the courtyard and the windows of the coachman's quarters were broken. In the harness-room were a few mouldering pieces of harness, and in every empty room some tiny scraps of evidence remained to show that the stables had once been alive. The corn bins were empty, but rotting sacks still lay piled in one corner. There was a rusty bit hanging on a nail in one of the loose-boxes, and in the coach-house itself the seats of a brougham were still stacked up, their torn velvet almost unrecognizable, a few lumps of smelly flock hanging from them like entrails.

The two girls crouched in the empty stable, in half-darkness. Bisto had produced a lump of pudding from her pocket and laid it on the floor a few yards away from them. The minutes went by and every now and again Bisto made a curious soft noise in her throat. I don't know where she learnt the lore which enabled her to get on friendly terms with wild creatures.

'Oh, let's give him up,' said Rachel impatiently.

'No, no,' whispered Bisto. 'We haven't seen him for ages. Perhaps he's hungry. He might even be too faint to walk.'

She was distressed. She loved Willy. There was a slight rustling in the corner. 'There he is,' she breathed.

A small brown creature scuttled across the floor, sniffed cautiously, inspected the food for a moment and then fell on it voraciously. It then picked up a huge lump of pudding and disappeared down its hole.

'Poor darling, how hungry he is! But he thinks of his wife and dear ones at home, his quiverful,' said Bisto, feelingly. 'He's much more unselfish than any human being.'

The rat reappeared and gnawed again for a few delicious moments, then half-dragged the remaining lump of suet towards its hole. It manoeuvred it to the entrance, propelling it with forefeet and snout, negotiated the hole successfully and disappeared with its booty. The girls rose and stretched. Bisto looked at her watch.

'Oh, lord,' she groaned. 'It's after three. We're late for prep.'

The mistress on duty wrote down their names as they went into the cloakroom. Bisto was crestfallen.

'Does that make me up to six points?' she asked.

66

'No, only five,' replied Rachel with irritation. She knew well enough that most of Bisto's bad points were gained in company with herself and too often through her fault, and she felt guilty. The climax came with the sixth point, which resulted in a spell of punishment drill. This to Rachel was no more than an hour's deprivation of liberty, but to Bisto it was torture.

As she sat down at her desk, Rachel saw Margaret looking at her with a sardonic smile. She threw a glance back which was intended to convey alliance. 'We're in this together,' she wanted to say. But Margaret ceased smiling and took up her pen. Obviously *she* had not been late for prep.

It was inevitable that Bisto should suffer. She attracted pain. Her unhappy, anxious face reflected the shadow of a harpy's wing for ever hovering over her, a creature which saw her downsitting and her uprising and spied out all her ways, quick to mark what she did amiss.

'It *was* the sixth point. I've got P.D.,' she said ruefully to Rachel the following evening. 'I shan't be able to come out tomorrow. I'll be on that awful block of concrete, being *tortured*. Will you go down and feed Willy? And then, after P.D., if there's anything left of me, I could come down and join you.'

'But I suppose I'll have to go out "on bounds",' said Rachel.

'You could easily put your name down with Margaret or one of the others, couldn't you?'

Week-end walks outside the park – 'on bounds' – had to be taken in groups of not less than three, and passes had to be obtained from the housemistresses. Margaret and Rachel had both, on several occasions, persuaded others to include their names on a pass, and then gone off secretly upon their

67

private occasions. It was an easy technique, though the consequences of such a deception, if found out, would have been serious. But both were delighted to take risks of this kind, Rachel even more than Margaret, for to Margaret it was largely a matter of indifference whether she were expelled, whereas to Rachel it was a deliberate risk, compatible with the physical risks she took to satisfy her physical strength. For Bisto to encourage such a thing showed the measure of her desperation. She could not face Saturday afternoon without Rachel. After P.D. was over, there was nothing for the victims to do but wander about the park or sit in their form-rooms. Others took this in their stride, but Bisto, broken by previous occasions, dreaded it almost as much as the P.D. which preceded it. She needed Rachel to restore her after an hour in the hands of Miss Christian Lucas, who took the punishment drill. Rachel agreed to fake a pass, and Bisto looked a little less tortured.

Although not a member of the triumvirate, Miss Lucas was bound to Chief by a personal tie. She was no mere employee. Her friendship with Delia Faulkner had been formed during the war, and it was in her house in Somerset that the school had been founded, and existed for three years before its growth necessitated the move to Bampfield. Miss Christian Lucas was tall and although only in her thirties had a shock of pure white hair. Her eyes, like Miss Gerrard's, were of a hard, piercing blue, but with a difference. The eyes of Miss Gerrard were like the eyes of God. They pierced through one's soul. They were moral eyes. However uncomfortable they made me feel, I never feared them as prying eyes, nor was there a hint of cruelty in them. They were terrible but just. I was afraid of her, as most of us were, but I believe that fear was the most wholesome emotion at

Bampfield. Miss Christian Lucas's eyes were the slightly bulging china-blue eyes of the sadist. They assumed a horrid magnitude and her face a hue of unhealthy purplish red when she was angry. But no one ever laughed at Miss Lucas. She was powerful not merely by virtue of her friendship in high places, but in her own right. She had the inner power of evil as I think I have never seen it in anyone else. She did me less harm personally than some others in authority at Bampfield, yet for her I feel a detestation untempered by pity.

I remember well my first meeting with her. It was the second day of my school career. The tall white-haired figure bore down upon me, an alarming figure – the blue eyes very prominent and glaring, the muscles taut and stringy, stretched over a frame of which flesh and skin seemed to have shrunk to a mere carapace.

'I am Miss Christian Lucas. What is your name?' asked the figure.

'Rachel Curgenven.'

'And where do you live, Rachel Curgenven?'

'At Sandhurst, Miss Lucas.'

'I see. At Sandhurst. Your father is in the army, no doubt?'

'No, Miss Lucas. He is a doctor.'

'Oh, a doctor.' (Air slightly chillier, but not cold, for doctoring was, after all, a profession, even if not so honourable a one as soldiering.)

'Have you brothers, Rachel?'

'Yes, I have three.'

'Ah, no doubt they will be at the Military College.'

'I'm afraid not –'

The eyes glared fiercely at me. The sinews of the neck were drawn as tight as a military strap. For a moment she seemed at a loss for words, so enormous was my family's crime in following peaceful professions. Then a gleam came into her eye and she said – quite seriously, I must emphasize, and without any jovial attempt to put me at my ease – 'You will have to be the soldier of the family, Rachel Curgenven.'

For drill we assembled outside the house on the flat sweep of the drive, surfaced with flints which cut one's gym-shoes to pieces. Unless it was actually pouring with rain, drill was always held there, or else on a piece of raised, bumpy concrete adjoining the school chapel. No matter whether the midday sun beat down upon our unprotected heads, or a westerly gale blew upon our shivering bodies, no matter whether frost sharpened the soft contours of the park, or (as was commoner) swathes of mist obscured the trees and the little round shrubberies, and marshy vapours filled our lungs as we *Breathed ... Deep! Breathed ... Deep!* drill must be held out of doors, for this was part of the toughening process of the system.

'Arms ... *Swing!* Arms ... *Swing!* Knees ... outward ... *Bend! Stretch! Bend! Stretch!*'

The commands echo in my mind still.

Miss Lucas's sadism found its fullest outlet in the punish-ment drill, which took place for one hour on Saturday afternoons on the grim slab of concrete immediately outside the chapel. This was roughly the size of a tennis court, and the concrete seemed to have been made by workmen infected with the same malignant humour as Miss Lucas, for it was rough and stony and full of unexpected holes and excres-cences designed to trip the unwary or fatigued offender. It did not improve Miss Lucas's temper that in having to conduct punishment drill she invariably missed every school match, and Miss Lucas was an ardent upholder of Bampfield's

70

honour on the games field. The exercises she chose, therefore, were designed to punish, and were pursued until the
unfortunate victims were almost dropping.

The drill was always preceded by an inquisition into the
reasons for which the punishment was being given, for Miss
Lucas liked to know what she was punishing. Suitably
scathing comments then accompanied her orders, individuals
being picked out by name, and the worst offenders sometimes given a harder and longer grilling. She always took
care to provide herself with a dossier on each child's origins
and family connection, and this affected her treatment of
individuals, her judgments being further reinforced by a
retentive memory which fastened up each misdemeanour
like a gobbet of meat in the thorny larder of the butcher-
bird. Bisto was especially the focus of Miss Lucas's sadistic
hate, for her father was only in the Marines, a service she
regarded as most inferior; and Bisto possessed, also, a quiet,
enduring temper which Miss Lucas interpreted as imper-
tinence.

Saturday was cold with the peculiar cold of Somerset
that is three parts damp, exhaled from the sodden earth and
spreading over the ground a layer of frigidity, a sub-atmo-
sphere which the soft, ineffectual winds of the district never
dispersed.

Margaret had suggested to Rachel going over to Stoke,
a village technically out of bounds, but dear to them both.
Rachel remembered her promise to Bisto and hesitated.

Margaret's temper was short these days. 'All right, all
right,' she said, 'I can take Rena. Go and smoke cigarettes
in the shrubberies and feed your silly rat. God, Rachel
Curgenven, you'll never grow up.'

Wounded, Rachel retorted: 'It's not that. Bisto's got

P.D. I promised I'd wait for her. You know how that brute treats her.'

'Don't be so sentimental about her. *Motherly* Rachel Curgenven, you're a fool. Kindness cuts no ice, and Bisto should be more careful, then she wouldn't get P.D. I'm going to Stoke.'

Margaret stalked away. Rena? thought Rachel bitterly. Beastly, slimy little snake.

Angry with Bisto for being the cause of a wasted afternoon, and hurt with Margaret for her easy contempt, Rachel bullied three of her weaker contemporaries into including her name on their pass and went down to the stables, with a pocketful of food for Willy. But the afternoon was ruined. Willy refused to come out, and Rachel waited in the gloomy harness-room, reading *Wuthering Heights*, in the fading daylight, and feeling more like Heathcliff with every page. When she found that it was more than half an hour since P.D. was over, she turned suddenly savage. Even Bisto had failed her.

Forgetting her deception over the pass, she went back into school and looked for her. Two or three forlorn girls, victims of Miss Lucas's recent persecution, hung about the empty, unwarmed classrooms. They stared at Rachel's dark, angry face with delighted curiosity.

'She'll murder Christian when she finds out,' whispered one, and Rachel, quick of hearing, turned on her.

'Finds out what?' she asked. 'Where's Bisto?'

'She fainted at P.D.'

'*Fainted?*'

'Yes, Christian had her walking round and round the concrete for hours with her hands above her head.'

'You little beast. Why didn't you tell me straight away?'

72

Rachel hit the child savagely, and sent it retreating with a whimper to its desk. Anger compelled her overgrown strength to displays of bullying, and the others watched anxiously to see what she would do next. But the habit of self-control was also strong. Ashamed of her outburst, Rachel walked away without another word and went up to Bisto's dormitory. Bisto was lying in bed, looking extremely pale.

'I'll go to Chief about this,' said Rachel, looking sternly down into the pleading, doglike eyes of Bisto.

'I wish you wouldn't,' said the victim miserably. 'They might find out about the pass, and it'll be too awful if they do. Go away, please, do.'

A melodious whistle was heard coming down the passage towards the dormitory. Rachel went over to the window and turned to face Chief who ignored her and walked swiftly over to Bisto.

'Miss Lucas tells me you fainted,' she said, and took up one of Bisto's hands.

'I'm all right,' said the Bampfield stoic.

Chief was silent for a moment, mentally selecting the appropriate speech for the occasion. Then she sat down on the edge of the bed in an infinitely graceful attitude.

'Punishment drill is not pleasant,' she began. 'It is not intended to be. You will find, as you go out into the world, that you often have to suffer what seems to you injustice and hardship. This world of ours, Bisto, this weary, wicked world, is a hard, uncompromising place. Why should Gud make it easy for us? He did not make it easy for His only Son. Here at Bampfield, we are trying to train you to take your place in Gud's world, Gud's just and terrible world. Miss Lucas is just. Very just. I have known her too long not to believe that she treated you with perfect justice.'

73

Hypnotized, Bisto heard these words without a tremor.

'But we are all of us, you and I, all of us, too weak at times to bear even justice. You need not feel ashamed that you fainted. Out of your moment of weakness you have gained strength. I am sure of that. I hope you understand me, Bisto.'

'Yes, Chief.'

'I have asked Miss Lucas to keep an eye on you.'

'Thank you, Chief.'

'As for you, Rachel, I believe you should not be in someone else's dormitory. You may stay with Bisto for another five minutes.'

Chief departed, her whistle retreating down the corridor, a melodious anthem after the sermon.

'God almighty!' said Rachel under her breath, swearing one of Margaret's oaths in her disgust.

CHAPTER TEN

Meanwhile the mind, for pleasure less
Withdraws into its happiness;
The mind, that recess where each kind
Doth straight its own resemblance find.
Yet it creates, transcending these
Far other worlds and other seas.
ANDREW MARVELL

THE fragile coat of rime stiffened over the long grass. Ice appeared in the sluggish meanderings of the stream. The whole envelope of atmosphere in which Bampfield lay embalmed suddenly clarified, and contours of the hills sharpened at the edges. It could now be seen that Moses was several trees, not one. The smoke from the home farm chimneys drifted up against the sallow green of the hill, and sounds became crystalline, stones dropped into a well: the high-pitched creak of a cart, a dog barking in distant cottages, and the birdlike notes of the church clock were carried through the resonant, frosty air into the windows of the school.

Rachel's perceptions became sharper, tauter, more distinct. The elements of the life she was living separated into recognizable patterns, like pictures of frost on glass. All that was distasteful to her at Bampfield assumed palpable outlines. She could no longer accept their once-soft, once-blurred contours. All that she loved and felt particular to herself, receded, diminished, behind a wall of glass, and she felt it beyond her reach. Bampfield, the real Bampfield, forced

75

itself upon her senses – a place of dank, ill-smelling corridors, of fetid little corners where girls whispered, a place where cruelty dwelt under the guise of discipline, and corruption beneath a mask of beauty and moral tone. She felt herself trapped like a bird in its icy reality, involved inevitably in the decay, the corruption, the loathesomeness beneath the fine, glassy surface. It was no longer possible to extract from it the different essences, the pleasures, stupidities, horrors, humours, and turn upon each a separate personality. All were, with herself, embalmed in a frigid, transparent pattern.

No more parodies came from her pen. Life did not seem laughable any more and she was too immature for satire. She spent most of her time in the library, where the imposition of silence made it unnecessary to speak to others. Her creative urge was over, spent in the translation of Virgil. That inner world of pleasure was sealed off for her. Fortunately, work for University entrance gave Rachel a special time-table which often involved working at different hours from her fellows, and she was relieved to get away from the form-room, from the distraction of twenty other living minds, and to walk alone through the building, past closed doors, behind which tired and reddened faces pored over exercise books. She was even able on occasions to miss games for coaching and get out for solitary walks in the park or gardens when others were still in class.

It was on one of these occasions, during bright and frosty weather, that she decided to discover for herself what it was that Margaret had found and never communicated. She might have done this before but for an enlarged sense of honour, which prevented her from intruding upon another's secret world. And always she had hoped that Margaret herself would tell her but she had never done so. She purloined the pliers from one of the gardeners' sheds and walked down the lime avenue towards the deserted stables till she was out of sight of the house. Then she turned across the stream by its lowest bridge and back to the shrubbery on the far side. There was no one about. The frosty rushes creaked under her shoes. She found the place where Margaret entered, and, to salve her conscience, selected another part of the palings, several yards away. It took her some time to get the wire cut and the palings out. She was not so practical as Margaret. At last it was done and she climbed through into dense undergrowth. She was in a thicket of overgrown shrubs, azalea and rhododendron mostly, their tough twisted trunks meshed in bramble and nettle. Through this she pushed her way with some difficulty, drawn towards the centre of the plantation only by her sense of direction. Shiny boughs of laurel brushed a green wound over her sleeve. For a moment she hesitated, pulled up by the world of school, in which stained or torn clothes must be explained, absences justified. Then an obstinate desire to force her way into the heart of the place gave her impetus, and thrusting aside the brown stringy creepers, she pushed on through the undergrowth.

She emerged into a strange, secret world, a clear blue sky above, willows, a lake, a coloured pagoda, and a tiny bridge – the world of a willow-pattern plate.

The park stream ran right through the centre of the large plantation, and in the heart of it had been created two pools big enough to sail a boat on, and indeed the poor relic of a punt still lay rotting in the boathouse. The pools lay close together and the stream that joined them had been divided into two courses, making a tiny, almost circular island between the lakes. Here stood a summerhouse, built like a Chinese pagoda, and reached by two bridges, one over each stream, highly ornamented in the oriental style so that the whole scene, viewed from the point where she stood, possessed the formal beauty of a Chinese plate, its rim the fringe of trees around the still, shallow pools.

Rachel crossed a creaking, dilapidated bridge, and went into the tiny pagoda. Bells were still hanging under the painted eaves, their copper green with age, shrill and fragile when she touched them with her hand. It was inhabited only by spiders. The floorboards were rotten, and covered with bird droppings, and the once bright paint was blistered and faded. The quiet pools, greened over with weed, never-disturbed, the dense overgrown shrubbery which hedged it from the world without, the incongruous oriental appearance of the pagoda and its bridges, created an indescribable air of secrecy and strangeness. She entered an exotic world where she breathed pure poetry. It had the symmetry of Blake's tiger. It was the green thought in a green shade.

She wandered slowly about, mapping it out in her mind. Its dereliction did not distress her. She was used to decay and ruin. The Chinese garden still offered, in its broken bridges and peeling cupola, the symbols of a precise pattern, a perfection greater than itself. Its complex image held within it a world of images, unfolding to the heart unending sequences of dream. Rachel realized now why Margaret, after visiting the garden again, had no wish to bring anyone else into it. To do so would be to reduce it to the status of a playground. It was not that. Entering it, one shed one's reality and partook of its charmed atmosphere, like the hero of a fairy tale who, on reaching the enchanted palace, hears music from the air, and from cups presented by invisible hands, drinks a paradisal wine.

A few days later, term ended. Reluctantly I went home. Home with its passions, its poverty, its wall of misunderstanding between parents and children, brothers and sisters, made more impenetrable by the blood which cemented it – home was a place that I dreaded. The countryside around it furnished a certain measure of escape, but it was not an invariable comfort to me. It lacked the familiarity of Bampfield and its clearly defined limits. In the countryside around my home I was adrift. I wandered and came up against no familiar fencing. One might, I felt at times as I walked alone through the hazel copses, one might walk for ever and out of the world. There was too weak a centrifugal force to hold me to the hub of this universe. Thus my walks at home, lacking security, lacking a sense of possession, were always a faint source of fear. I was compelled to take them, yet I half hated them. They were the wrong sort of solitude, a solitude imposed rather than a solitude sought. I did not withdraw, as I did at Bampfield, into a secret world. I ran out into a desert to escape from home, and explored the unfamiliar with a kind of desperate hope that I would find in it something that would reassure me. When the end of the holidays came, I returned to Bampfield with a readiness that grieved my parents.

Travelling down in the train through the well-known landscape, now sodden with January rain, viewing the sheets of flood water over the Somersetshire meadows, I drew towards me the picture of Bampfield, its features, its touch, its smell, as if I were pulling towards me, by the hand, some loved and familiar figure. Resting serenely in my mind was the image of the Chinese garden. The disgust and tedium I had felt at the end of the previous term had been exorcised by absence. At the heart of Bampfield lay a world private to myself, and one which was so powerfully present to my thoughts that I did not need to visit it at once. It shed its enchanted light over those aspects of school for which I had recently felt so much detestation, and I found myself accepting again the life I had temporarily lost.

CHAPTER ELEVEN

O hours of childhood,
hours when behind the figures there was more
than the mere past, and when what lay before us
was not the future! We were growing, and sometimes
impatient to grow up, half for the sake
of those who'd nothing left but their grown-upness.
Yet when alone we entertained ourselves
With everlastingness.

RAINER MARIA RILKE

'How you are enjoying yourself, aren't you?' said Margaret sardonically, when she and Rachel had lingered behind in the form-room after the bell had gone. It was some weeks after the beginning of term, and the first time they had spoken to each other except in the presence of others. Rachel was silent. She did not feel *en rapport* with her this term. The brilliant beam of Margaret's personality was turned in another direction, and Rachel was too glad to be back at Bampfield to be wounded by her apparent defection and too occupied to make the effort to get back once more on to intimate terms with her.

'Go on – ' goaded Margaret – 'you and your childish pleasures. I don't know how you bear this place, Rachel, let alone enjoy it. All you do is fool about with Bisto, feeding rats and writing silly parodies.'

'I haven't written any parodies this term. I'm trying to write a play, in fact.'

'A play?' Margaret's eyes lit up. 'Why the hell didn't you tell me?'

'I didn't think you'd be interested. You seem occupied.'

'With Rena, I suppose you mean?'

'Well, yes, I suppose I do.'

'And you don't like her, do you?'

'No, I can't stand her.'

'She's not everybody's cup of tea.'

'Perhaps Bisto isn't either, but I happen to like her.'

'That's different,' said Margaret.

'I don't see why.'

'Tell me about your play. That's more interesting than Bisto or Rena.'

'I can't begin now, we'll be sent up soon.'

'It's only Punch on duty,' said Margaret, and went on eagerly, 'look here, let's go up now, and meet later on. We haven't done that for ages.'

'It wasn't my fault,' said Rachel stubbornly.

'Oh, don't go on about it,' said Margaret. 'All right, it was mine. Now are you satisfied?'

Punch opened the door. She smiled blandly at them, as she usually did upon wrongdoers who were doing exactly the sort of things she liked doing herself.

'I hate to interrupt you,' she said, 'since conversation is one of the most rewarding arts and I like to know that you practise it. But rules, alas, are rules.'

'I'm sorry,' muttered Margaret as they went up the staircase in semi-darkness. 'Come, all the same, Rachel.'

'Where?'

'I suppose it's too cold to go out?'

'I should think so.'

'It'll have to be a music cell then. Number nine at the end. At ten o'clock. Will you bring the play?'

'Well, we shan't be able to have the light on.'

'I'll bring a torch.'

'All right. At ten. Don't go to sleep.'

'I shan't go to sleep,' answered Margaret and paused in the gallery. All along it were engravings and reproductions of paintings, many of them of the Pre-Raphaelite school. They had stopped under one which depicted Cleopatra riding in her barge. Margaret looked at it intently.

'Rena is like Cleopatra,' she said slowly, 'like Cleopatra sitting on her burnished throne.'

Never having given a thought to the picture before, Rachel looked hard at it, and saw that there was, indeed, a likeness.

'Don't you think she's beautiful?' asked Margaret, rather feverishly.

Not knowing whether she referred to Cleopatra or Rena, Rachel answered cautiously: 'Oh, well, I suppose so.'

'You're studying classics,' said Margaret, contemptuously, 'but you don't seem to have acquired the Greek attitude to physical beauty.'

'I'm not studying Greek,' answered Rachel with maddening precision. 'It's Latin.'

'Latin,' said Margaret in anger. 'Yes, that's what you are. Very Roman. You love order, and routine and discipline and ... and ... hardships. You're like Antony who drank the stale of horses. I don't believe you know the meaning of pleasure, except perhaps brutal Roman pleasures.'

'Shut up,' said Rachel angrily.

'I don't care. You're a pure Roman. I suspect you have secret vices. You probably torture Bisto when you go off with her to your stupid secret hiding-places. Disgusting, Roman Empire tortures. I've read all about them.'

In the distance the long-drawn notes of Chief's whistling,

never of any known tune, reached them. Margaret walked quickly away. Rachel stood for a moment staring down over the curved banisters into the well of the hall. A soft padding of footsteps and another burst of whistling. She ran down the stairs and offered her shoulder to Chief, and they mounted the stairs together, side by side.

'Thank you, my dear Curgenven. But it's late. Oughtn't you to be undressed?'

'I'm sorry. I ought. I was thinking.' (Certain appeal to Chief.)

'Do you often stand in the gallery to think?'

'Sometimes.'

'It's a beautiful gallery, isn't it?'

Chief paused, and leaning heavily on Rachel's shoulder, swept a slow gaze down the curved balustrading and into the shadows of the hall.

'What were you thinking about? Don't tell me if you don't want to. I'm not probing.'

As one adult to another, Rachel took a step forward out of childhood.

'It's about a play. I'm writing one.'

Chief turned and looked into her face. Rachel could have said nothing that would more have fired her spirit.

'A play!' she repeated with delight. 'Rachel Curgenven, you renew my youth. Will you tell me about it? Not now necessarily, but some time?'

'Yes, of course, Chief.'

'And show it to me, I hope?'

'To you, first of all,' said Rachel, capitulating to the moment's emotion.

They were in the gallery now, under the picture of Cleopatra.

'Do you think she really looked like that?' asked Rachel suddenly.

'Who?'

'Cleopatra.'

'The painter has done his best, but Shakespeare did better.' Chief began walking very slowly down the gallery towards her own wing, which opened off one end of it.

'The barge she sat in,' began Chief, 'I wonder if I can remember it ...

> ' "The barge she sat in, like a burnish'd throne,
>   Burn'd on the water; the poop was beaten gold,
>   Purple the sails, and so perfumed, that
>   The winds were love-sick with them, the oars were
>   silver,
>   Which to the tune of flutes kept stroke, and made
>   The water which they beat to follow faster,
>   As amorous of their strokes. For her own person,
>   It beggar'd all description ..." '

Her senses held by the poetry, Rachel's truant mind played with the tempting hope that she would be able to evade going to her dormitory at all. To stay with Chief until ten and then go down to the music cells to meet Margaret – a water-tight excuse handed to her gratis, if she should be caught walking the corridors still dressed at ten o'clock. With simple cunning, just as they came to Chief's outer door, she said, 'Is it very presumptuous of me to write a play in blank verse?'

'I don't think so,' said Chief. 'You have the stuff of poetry in you. Shakespeare has no monopoly on blank verse. You know Clemence Dane's plays well enough, and that's blank verse of the first order. What is your play about?'

'It's a play about the horrors of marriage,' said Rachel, impulsively.

Chief stopped and thought over the words. 'Let's hear what the horrors of marriage are,' she said, and they entered the warm firelight together.

It was one of many occasions when Rachel had spent the evening in Chief's room. In the winter there would be a roaring fire of logs lighting up the great Tudor room, with its fine moulded ceiling and plaster swags on the walls. The sybaritic comfort of it was a welcome inducement to sit there talking to her, often for hours. Then, long after the proper bed-time, when the rest of the school was asleep in the draughty dormitories, Rachel would be dismissed, and would walk slowly down the darkened corridors, savouring every moment of her solitude.

Yet now, when it came to the point, Rachel found that she could not talk easily of her play. Somehow the sentiments propounded in it in a mixture of Shakespeare and Gilbert Murray were inexpressible in common speech. And the roots of the play, her loathing of home, and disgust with her parents' version of wedded life, together with the deeper though virtually unrecognized disgust which accompanied her dawning knowledge of sexual love, could only be buried under the cloak of a myth. She could use her own reactions but not her home itself. Loyalty prevented her from revealing the source of her disgust.

'It's about Clytemnestra,' she said unemotionally.

'Who killed Agamemnon with an axe, I seem to remember,' said Chief. 'Remind me of the rest of the story.'

'Agamemnon went off to the Trojan wars. He sacrificed Iphigenia – to persuade the Gods to give him a fair wind.'

'Yes,' said Chief. 'I remember, of course.'

86

' " Her spirit is fled,
Her fair body taken
Within the tomb.
Do her eyes awaken
Some light in the gloom
In the halls of the dead?" '

It was one of Rachel's own poems that she quoted. Chief
was susceptible to the strains of Gilbert Murray. She had
praised the poem, and it had stayed in her retentive memory.

'How wonderful of you to remember it,' said Rachel,
struck secretly with far more wonder at her own poetic
powers that had given birth to such a lyric.

'It is one of the best poems you have written. I hope the
play is as good. Has it any lyrics?'

'Yes, choruses.'

'Euripides? Not a bad model,' observed Chief.

There was a brief silence. Rachel did not feel able to say
anything more about it. For Chief it must be the finished
product. Work in progress could be discussed with Margaret
alone. Her momentary flash of self-assurance after hearing
the Iphigenia lyric was swallowed up in the darkness of inner
doubt. Was it, after all, so very good, that poem? It was
slight, it was shallow, a verbal skimming over the surface.
Even Chief's voice could not give it wings. But for her play,
Clytemnestra, she felt she had plumbed the depths herself.
Accumulated bitterness and loathing had been drawn up
from them and the Greek legend was no more than a vessel
for this bitter well-water.

Chief's sensitivity was acute. She would not press Rachel
to tell her anything more. She set out to restore Rachel's
confidence by bringing out from the bookshelves the hard-

covered notebook in which Rachel had written out her translation of Virgil's Book Eight for Miss Burnett, the previous term.

'This has given me great pleasure,' she began. 'I'd like to read you a piece of it. It reads well aloud.' Her beautiful well-kept hands turned over the pages slowly. 'Yes, this passage about the journey down the river.

' "Throughout the day and night they strain the oars,
  Winding along still reaches, while the trees
  Cast dappled shade below; the quiet stream
  Bears them along between the leafy woods." '

Rachel settled herself more easily into the deep hearth rug and felt the heat from the piled logs flare up against her cheeks. The firelight winked against Chief's empty wine glass and in the amber eyes of her giant Alsatian. Fascinated, Rachel listened to her voice, lending an enchantment to the rough blank verse of her translation and restoring her to the days of confidence, during the last term, when she had written it. It was an intoxicating experience.

'There,' said Chief. 'There. It's good, Rachel Curgenven. You will write more, and write better. I'm certain of it. But you must keep to the lyrical vein. This translation is, perhaps, a kind of exercise. But it's your own imagination you must explore, not Virgil's.'

She was not always so perceptive for she was too dominated by her own emotional needs. Perhaps at that moment the isolated poles of being which were Chief and Rachel, touched and struck off, in the electric atmosphere, a single illuminating flash. It was more than the warmth of encouragement. It was the rare self-illuminating light that flickers occasionally at one touch of an alien hand.

Rachel said good-night with the usual formal handshake. It was twenty minutes to ten. She lingered for a moment.

'Would you give me permission to do something irregular?' she asked.

'What, my dear Rachel? By irregular, I suppose you mean against the rules?'

'Well, not exactly. Beyond – outside the rules,' said Rachel.

'What is it then?'

'May I walk once round the house, outside?'

'It's very cold, and I imagine very dark.' Chief walked over to the window and pulled back the heavy curtain. The February night was illuminated by a brilliant full moon.

'It's like daylight,' said Rachel, 'and I can put a coat on. I don't mind the cold, anyway.'

Rarely did Chief fail to respond to a suggestion such as this.

'You may go with my blessing,' she said, giving with her hand an exquisite gesture of dismissal.

Rachel went quickly down the turret stairs. She found her coat and let herself out of the back door into the night. Above her, a pale grey sky stretched over the hills, raddled with cloud. The walls of the house wore a sheeted, ghostly look. The light wind that was pargeting the cloud above her, stirred the leaves of the great magnolia near the house.

Fearful but enthralled, Rachel walked slowly through the lower path of the pleasure garden, out on to the back drive which led down to the stables. She could see clearly the black mass of shrubbery which held the Chinese garden. She felt a wild desire to see it by moonlight, to evoke from it an even greater mystery and enchantment; its weed-haunted pool a mirror for stars, its pagodas and bridges harbouring unfathomable shadows, drained of colour. Normal childhood fears overcame her. Should she persuade Margaret to go with her, who knew the garden as well as she did, or better? She hurried round the house, over the loose gravel, and in at the still-open front door. There was no one about. It was nearly ten. Quietly, she crossed the hall and let herself into the back corridors. The music cell was still empty, and she stood there in the darkness, her heart beating, her eyes filled with the pattern of the garden, silver and shadow.

But Margaret did not come. Standing alone, Rachel's exaltation ebbed away. The scents of night faded from her nostrils. The cold bloom of the night air vanished from her skin. The immediate smell of fungoid decay, the close touch of stale air in the deserted room, slowly enveloped her. With a sudden impulse, she left the music cell, and crossing the hall, let herself out of the front door once again.

She turned away from the house and began to walk quickly across the grass towards the distant shrubbery. There was no need now to go to the bridge by the longer and more discreet route. A few lights still shone from the upstairs windows and she fortified herself against her fears by looking back at them from time to time. Then a kind of bravado began to take possession of her. The shrubbery enclosing the Chinese garden loomed larger, and her physical terror at its black density increased with every step, but to counteract it there grew within her a stubborn determination to meet its challenge and a romantic conviction that the garden was hers only if she could win it through this night ordeal. When she reached the palings she realized with momentary relief that she had no pliers, hesitated, even turned back towards the house, and then faced the palings again, stiff with fear, almost weeping. She pulled the loosened strands of wire apart and pushed her way into the undergrowth. Her progress to the centre became an ordeal. The Chinese garden assumed the stature of a spiritual prize. She pursued her way doggedly and the purgative property of pure terror stripped her mind of its earlier associations. Its bravado, its romanticism, its secrecy, were pared away, leaving in their place something so intimate, so powerful in its impact, that her final emergence upon the edge of the dark lake, with its silent pagoda and waiting willows, was like an embrace.

When Rachel left the garden, she was too exhausted to combat the simple, primitive panic of trees and darkness. She ran back to the house as though fiends were after her and climbed in by a form-room window. Lights were out now. The house was full of shadows and creaking. She went up by the back stairs past the corridor where Rena slept. She paused at a landing and looked along the passage and saw with surprise a figure standing at one of the windows. For a moment she backed against the wall, fearing to be seen. Whoever it was turned to go, and for a second her head was silhouetted against the window. It was Margaret. Rachel called out in a whisper.

They stood at the window, looking out over the roofs of the kitchen quarters at the back of the house.

'I couldn't come,' Margaret said, defensively. 'I got caught by someone. I'm awfully sorry. Did you wait for me?' And without waiting for Rachel's reply, she went on quickly: 'I say, you're still dressed, and you're wet. Have you been *out*? By yourself?'

'Yes.' Rachel felt dazed. 'I waited for you in the cell and then I went out.' She did not say where.

They stood in silence. Neither knew what to say to the other. Both had come from an incommunicable experience. Both were trying to adjust themselves to the world of school, which was reasserting its dominion over them with every moment they stood there.

'God, you will catch it if anyone finds you still dressed,' said Margaret. 'I can say I was just going to the lavatory, but you can't.'

'You're a good way off from your room,' observed Rachel.

'I shall say I like the lavatories on this floor better than the ones on mine,' retorted Margaret, with a touch of her old sardonic humour. 'Oh, damn, there *is* someone. Clear off. I'll deal with her.'

Miss Burnett slouched into the light, cigarette between her lips. Rachel had stood her ground, unwilling to go.

'You're up late,' observed Miss Burnett. 'Why?'

'I was being excused,' answered Margaret, 'and I ran into Rachel. She's been with Chief. Good night, Rachel. Good night, Miss Burnett.' Margaret started to go.

'Wait a moment,' said Miss Burnett, 'why down here?'

Margaret gave a conspiratorial grin. 'Oh well, it gives me an opportunity to stretch my legs. It's so boring in bed when you can't sleep.'

Miss Burnett was close to Rachel now and could see that her hair was damp. No longer interested in Margaret, who was slowly walking away towards the stairs, she caught hold of the other and turned her fully into the light.

'You've been with Chief?'

'Yes.'

'Your hair's very damp.'

'I've been out for a walk. Chief said I could.'

'Chief gave you permission – at this time of night in February?' repeated Miss Burnett incredulously.

'Yes, she did really, Miss Burnett. Only ... I wish you wouldn't say anything.'

'Why? Because it isn't true?' asked Miss Burnett, her cigarette glowing in the dim light, and revealing a mocking expression on her face.

'No. It *is* true. She did give me permission, but I was out rather longer than I meant to be.'

'You're very cold,' said Miss Burnett. 'Your hair's soaking. Where have you been. You, and I suppose Margaret. Not smoking in my chicken houses?'

'No, not there, and Margaret wasn't with me. Please, Miss Burnett, don't tell Chief. She mightn't give me permission again if she knew how late I'd been.'

'We shall be allies, Rachel,' answered Miss Burnett, stubbing out her cigarette on the window sill. 'What was Margaret doing here, then?'

'Oh, she was really just going to be excused. It was only an accident our meeting.'

'It's a thin story,' she said, leaning back against the wall and surveying Rachel in the half light coming in through the window. 'A damned thin story.'

'But it is true, honestly.'

'Are you very fond of Margaret?' asked Miss Burnett, suddenly leaning forward nearer Rachel.

'Oh well, I like her,' answered Rachel defensively.

'Why don't you ... let her ... ' Miss Burnett hesitated and turned the sentence round another way. 'I think you ought to see less of her.'

A feeling of rebellious hatred for Bampfield and for Miss Burnett's sudden volte-face came over Rachel.

'Margaret and I hate this place,' she said savagely. 'That's why we're friends. We *both* hate it. It's a prison. I thought at least *you'd* understand and leave us alone, but ... '

'I suppose I sometimes remember that I am one of your teachers, and responsible for your welfare,' said Miss Burnett drily.

'I don't want you to remember. I want to be free.'

'You can't be,' said Miss Burnett. 'No one is.'

Rachel could feel tears rising in her eyes, and leaving the window she half ran back to her room and undressed and crept between the ice-cold sheets to abandon herself to transports of grief.

CHAPTER TWELVE

What we changed was innocence for innocence; we knew not
The doctrine of ill-doing, nor dream'd
That any did.
SHAKESPEARE

NEXT day, Margaret wanted to know what Miss Burnett
had said the night before, and was relieved to find that she
had not threatened to report Rachel, and had, apparently,
accepted the excuse for her own presence on the landing.
Rachel later saw her conveying this news to Rena, to the
obvious delight of both. But Margaret displayed no further
curiosity about that evening and offered no fuller explanation of her failure to come to the music cell. She appeared,
in fact, to avoid Rachel as far as possible, and at chance
meetings her face assumed an amiable, withdrawn expression. She made bantering remarks that glanced away so
quickly that any real conversation was impossible. Sometimes, in the evenings, Rachel saw her and Rena flitting
down the stone corridors to the music cells, and – like any
other adolescent – she felt herself, rather bitterly, passed
over. She was surprised, therefore, when Margaret gripped
her arm one Sunday evening after chapel, and whispered –
'Come out in the grounds with me. Please –' in tones of
urgency.

It was fine, and the cold air hardly mattered to children
who had access to so many secret places. By mutual consent
they went to Miss Burnett's chicken room, a wooden shed

in which were stored the bins of meal. The soft mounds of toppings accommodated them very comfortably. Margaret produced a packet of cigarettes, and they settled down, side by side. It seemed like old times and Rachel felt touched and flattered.

'You old devil,' she said affectionately. 'Why didn't you come to the music cell that night? I waited for half an hour, and I'd had such an evening with Chief ... I was aching to tell you about it.'

'Were you?' said Margaret, evasively.

She was more enigmatical than ever. In the darkness, even her masklike face could not be seen.

'Well, why didn't you come?' pursued Rachel, pulling happily on her cigarette. 'I was angry at the time.'

'It was Rena, I suppose. She wanted me. I wouldn't have told you that, but you're about the only person in this prison who would be likely to understand.'

Rachel felt that she understood perfectly well. She herself had a strong conscience about Bisto and had on occasion given up something she wanted to do far more, in order to be with her or keep a promise to her.

'Have you read this?' asked Margaret suddenly. She held a newspaper cutting and played the light of her torch on it. The sixth form common-room took several newspapers, including *The Times*. I don't think any of us read the news. Some read the sporting columns – we were a great school for the manly game of cricket – and I at least read the book reviews. It was among these that I had read one day at the beginning of that term a full column review of Radclyffe Hall's novel, *The Well of Loneliness*. I wondered then what all the fuss was about. It seemed an important book, but I could not quite see why. My technical knowledge of sex was too meagre to enable me to relate what little I knew to the reviewer's account of the novel. Now here was that very same cutting in Margaret's hand.

'Have you read it?' she asked. 'The book, I mean.'

'No, have you?'

'I haven't yet, but I'm going to. Anyway, if you've read the review you know what it's about.'

Unsure, Rachel said nothing.

'How damned unfair it is – ' Margaret went on – 'the way you can't live with someone you want, without everyone interfering and making your life hell. All anyone thinks about is marriage.'

'Well, I haven't read the book,' began Rachel. Her ignorance handicapped her badly, and she wanted to get away from a conversation, the implications of which were vague and disturbing. She thought of her play.

'Why should anyone *want* to marry?' she asked. 'It's just a chain. In fact, that's what my play is about.'

Here at last was the opportunity to talk to Margaret about *Clytemnestra*. She felt she had been rather adroit, and was about to embark happily upon the theme of the play, when Margaret cut in. 'I'm not talking about ordinary marriage. I'm not interested in it. It's only got one purpose – the procreation of children. I read the marriage service the other day, and I know all about it. And I don't want children.'

'Marriage,' said Rachel pontifically, her mind still on Clytemnestra's marital troubles, 'marriage is compulsory and licensed adultery. That's what I'm trying to say in *Clytemnestra*. It's about her free and glorious love for Aegisthus.'

'What's *Clytemnestra*? I never heard of it.'

'My play,' said Rachel impatiently.

'Oh, yes.' Margaret hesitated. 'I *do* want to hear about it, of course, but let me ask you something first – you might put it in your play, anyway. Why is everybody so dead set on *marriage*? Don't you think we ought to be free to live our own lives without society interfering with us?'

'Of course I do,' said Rachel. 'I keep telling you – that's what the play is about. The essence of love is that it should be free.'

'Nobody thinks that – or very few.'

'All the great writers thought it,' said Rachel sweepingly. 'You should read Shelley.'

'I hate Shelley,' replied Margaret promptly. 'He was soft and fat and white, like a snail without a shell.'

'He wasn't,' retorted Rachel. 'You wouldn't say that if you'd read *Prometheus Unbound*.'

'Well, he looked like that.' Margaret sounded sulky. 'And he had sordid love affairs and some poor fool drowned herself for love of him.'

'Well, why not? It was noble of her. I'd drown myself for someone like Shelley.'

'I wouldn't,' answered Margaret. 'I'd only drown myself for someone really worth while … for someone really beautiful that I felt I couldn't … I couldn't live without.'

'Like Rena?' asked Rachel, hardly knowing why she had put the question.

Margaret let out a long hiss of breath, as though she had been holding it in tensely for some moments.

'Like Rena,' she said. 'You'd think Chief would understand, wouldn't you? But she and the others, they're always trying to separate us. Georgie Murrill wouldn't sign my pass last Saturday. Rena and I were going to Colverton, and we'd put Audrey Parrish down a third, though we were going to get rid of her, of course, and Georgie crossed the pass through and made Rena go with that ghastly Anderton crowd and Audrey and me go with Ann Ashley and her party. God knows what right people like Georgie Murrill have to interfere.'

'Oh, they're always trying to separate people,' said Rachel. 'They don't like me being so friendly with you.'

'I know,' said Margaret. 'But somehow, not Chief. She's different. She'd understand, and what's more, she's got courage. She doesn't care what the world thinks.'

'I don't see why you're so worried,' said Rachel, 'you seem to see plenty of Rena in spite of them all.'

Margaret shrugged her shoulders, as though dismissing the subject.

'Oh, it'll work out,' she said lightly. 'I think I miss your scintillating conversation, Rachel. I grow old and think too much. I find myself discontented.' She was her old half-mocking self. 'Divine discontent.'

'God, that's what I feel,' said Rachel at once, putting her cigarette out. 'If only I could write something worth while.'

'You will,' said Margaret, 'I'm sure you will. You're the only person in this damned hole – I keep telling you – you're the only person who isn't utterly ordinary. You make it bearable.'

There was a moment's pause. Almost without intending it, Rachel heard herself say, as though she were unable to leave the subject alone, 'What about Rena?'

'Rena? *She* doesn't make Bampfield bearable. Sometimes I even hate her. I do tonight. I sometimes despise you, when you play the fool and fritter away your talents on parodies, but I never *hate* you.'

'You seem very thick with Rena, if you hate her.'

Margaret drew on the last remnant of her cigarette, lighting up for a moment her dark, intense eyes, and strong jutting nose. 'Don't *you* think she's fascinating?' she asked. 'I do.'

Rachel remained silent.

'Let's go back,' said Margaret abruptly. 'I feel awful – melancholy mad. I could cut my throat. Play something to me before we go to bed. I don't want to go up yet. I can't face ... well, I can't face it. I'd like to sleep out in one of these corn bins, but I suppose those bloody prefects would find out and raise the hue and cry. Let's go in and you play me some Bach, Rachel. There's just time, if we hurry.'

'Why do you always want Bach?' asked Rachel curiously, whose own tastes at this time ran to the Romantics.

'He's another world,' said Margaret.

'Not Bampfield, you mean?'

'Not Bampfield, not anywhere. He's outside me and you and Rena and the whole blasted universe. I wish I could play the piano. I'd play nothing but Bach. Everything falls into place in his music. It's the only music I like. Strong and intellectual. Above ordinary feeling.'

'I don't think Bach's unfeeling,' said Rachel.

'No, not unfeeling, but not full of ordinary down-in-the-mud feelings. Not all messed up with feelings for one particular person.'

'Oh, well,' said Rachel, uncomprehendingly. Her playing of Bach was largely the result of technical necessity and she infinitely preferred Beethoven's slow movements. She sat down at the piano and watched with a certain wonder the dark unrest of Margaret's face change almost to serenity as she played.

CHAPTER THIRTEEN

All my stars forsake me,
And the night winds shake me,
Where shall I betake me?
ALICE MEYNELL

I WOULD have called myself happy at Bampfield, yet looking
back on it over the span of many years, I can only regret that
I was not miserable during my time there. It would have
been more creditable in me, for my happiness came from
tainted sources. Bampfield gave me things which I thought
I wanted and imagined to be valuable. It enveloped me in an
atmosphere which I believed to be the purest ether. It so
conditioned most of us who were there that we thrived
on it, as plants and animals will thrive in quite unnatural
surroundings if they are habituated to them early enough.
Indeed, I found it difficult to breathe the air of the common
world when I emerged, and it took me years to adapt my
spiritual lungs to it.

Yet Bampfield was not one of those schools (often
pilloried in the national press and in novels) which endeavour
to turn out their pupils to a set mould. We were not,
despite the military nature of some of the discipline,
'Mädchen in Uniform'. Nor did we emerge as recognizable
types, as is certainly the case in some well-known girls'
boarding schools. The curious mixture of freedom and
restraint, the iron discipline combined with startling
breaches of rule in the interests of individuals, the almost

adult responsibility we were given as prefects, together with the ripe eccentricity of so many of those in authority over us – all this might have been a good preparation for life, in fact, in some ways it was. But the regime acted upon at least some of us like one of those powerful, selective weed-killers – certain facets of the personality were destroyed or driven under, while others were allowed to swell to monstrous almost grotesque proportions. In my own character, Bampfield encouraged just those elements which were to prove least valuable when I grew older, and it checked, diverted and all but destroyed the elements which I later discerned as best in me.

What I learned was detrimental – to trust without discrimination, to expect too much both of people and life, to surrender my personality, my inmost thoughts and feelings, too readily to the demand of others. Not until years afterwards did I learn that such a surrender leaves one no retreat. And even while I was, as I imagined, happy, the precariousness of my content was becoming evident. I look back on a Rachel Curgenven obstinately proclaiming to herself a happiness which was belied in every direction.

As the cold, rain-driven term went on, the surface security afforded by the rigid routine satisfied only a part, and that a diminishing one, of Rachel's personality. Her own nature, her deepening perceptions, would have brought dissatisfaction in the end, but the process was intensified by her preoccupation with the adult problems of love and marriage with which she was attempting to grapple in her play of Clytemnestra. Ignorant, inexperienced and prejudiced by home circumstances, this might have been no more than an adolescent malaise, but Margaret, with her cryptic remarks, forced the whole problem on to a more immediate plane.

What had been part theorizing, part fortuitous circumstance, took on the intensity of a near personal experience.

Conversation with Margaret usually had a disturbing effect upon Rachel, and the more so now when such conversations were rare. Phrases, undercurrents of meaning in Margaret's casual words, returned to trouble her mind again and again, and ruffled the smooth surface of her precarious Bampfield contentment. Her chance meeting with Margaret that night, after she had failed to keep the appointment at the music cell, and the general lack of rapport between the two of them, nagged at the back of her mind. She found her creative urge deserting her, was certain she would never write poetry again, felt out of love with herself and with her play. Her mind remained full of questionings but she could not have discussed them with anyone. She found a certain peace in Georgie Murrill's room, talking about house affairs, playing Beethoven duets, and discussing history. But she was wary, unable to surrender herself readily to the offered warmth; prickly, given to sudden moods, and displays of temper, which provoked the schoolmistress in Georgie, and ended in prim reprimands or curt dismissals. Rachel would then sulk. The *rapprochement* with Margaret was short-lived. There was no quarrel. Margaret simply did not seek her company, and Rachel was too proud to ask for it. At brief moments, Margaret would speak a few words to her, and the old note of intimacy was there, reinforced by an undercurrent of urgency to which Rachel would have responded had she known what response to make. But Margaret, always enigmatic, was doubly so now. She treated Rachel to a kind of intermittent confederacy, but in what she was a confederate, Rachel did not as yet know. It was an incomprehensible and unsatisfying alliance, the terms of which were completely beyond her.

It was then, almost as an experiment, that Rachel turned to religion. In the spring term candidates were prepared for confirmation and instruction had already begun. For two years Rachel had stubbornly refused to have anything to do with this, and had paraded her scepticism. Now she went to Chief and asked if it was too late to start the classes. Chief, delighted at this volte-face, allowed her to join them. Bampfield was a school centralized on God. We were made aware of this and derived from it, probably, a part of our security. The prospectus paid lip-service to 'Christian principles', 'A strong sense of religion', and few parents had the acumen to probe deeply into what was really meant by a phrase like 'The Principal believes that a Christian foundation in education is essential.'

When the school moved to this large Somersetshire house, the Head's first act was to build a school chapel. It was a long, low asbestos erection, jutting out from the side of the house, in close proximity to the school lavatories and kitchen premises. No more than the sanctuary itself was consecrated. The rest of the building was only dedicated. We were told that this had been done in order that we need not wear hats and our voices be lost in the brims, but I see now that it was only one of the many indirect attacks upon our femininity. It was usual for girls to wear hats in chapel but we were not girls. We were public school boys and therefore did not wear hats.

Schools of Bampfield's size could hardly have supported a permanent chaplain, but only one visiting clergyman was permitted to take services. He was the uncle of one of the staff, Miss Naylor, and he was rarely allowed to officiate except at Holy Communion. Morning and evening services on Sunday were taken by Chief, but even she did not dare arrogate to herself the right to administer the sacrament. She was very human in her desire to preach. She went just that much further than most clergymen manqués – she built herself a pulpit and a chapel to put round it. Nor do I blame her. What would I not give to preach – a long, meaty doctrinal sermon, or a fiery polemic against the wickedness of the world, and the certainty of hell for those upon whom I cast my glaring, impassioned, prejudiced eye; or a closely-knit piece of sophistry, as neatly fitted as a mosaic, on some obscure text, such as, 'And we were in our own sight as grasshoppers.'

In the school chapel, Sunday after Sunday, Chief played her favourite role. Her early years as an actress were a sound qualification for her assumption of clerical dignity. She had evolved her own ritual for our service, which, as the prospectus proclaimed, was undenominational. It was certainly this. Chief's ritual was as elaborate as the genuflecting and biretta-doffing of the Romans, and consisted of a great deal of play with her mortar-board, donning it here, doffing it there; and of gestures appropriate to certain points in the service, such as the taking of the offertory, when, at a moment nicely timed to coincide with the end of the collection, she rose from her seat (she usually sat through the hymns), took her mortar-board from the child behind her, hitched her royal blue hood round her shoulders, and walked towards the altar rails. When she reached them, she put on her mortar-board with an infinitely graceful gesture, and stood for a moment in front of the altar, greeting the Almighty. She then fetched the plate, and even the taking of the brass dish from its little table was done with such grace of outstretched arms and hands, that you might have expected her to dance back with it like Isadora Duncan. She would glance down the chapel to see what row the collectors were at and would time her movements so well with theirs that she would always arrive at the top of the altar steps just as they were embarking on their perambulation up the aisle. This gave her long enough, but not too long, to stand there waiting for them. I can see her very clearly, every detail of her face and clothes, as I saw her for six years on Sundays, while she waited for the collectors to reach her, and, the hymn finished, the harmonium droned its way rather inexpertly through a variety of keys in which, from time to time, the original tune of the collection hymn emerged gasping and half-drowned in the welter of harmony.

Chief's sermons revolved round the theme of the world, the flesh and the devil, and the paramount importance of self-control in combating these adversaries. The New Testament was taken as a convenient handbook of simple stories illustrative of the virtues of self-discipline. Jesus was treated as a glorified Head Prefect of our school. He was presented to us as more human than ourselves, but, we were given to understand, His extraordinary powers of self-control (of which one of the highlights was the forty days in the wilderness, and the crowning achievement His three hours on the Cross) gave Him the capacity to perform wonders which appeared to His contemporaries of supernatural origin. Thus were the miracles disposed of. Perhaps there is some truth in all this, but not, I think, sufficient truth. Small wonder that old Canon Naylor was only permitted to take the Communion service. These mysteries were fool-proof, required no verbal interpretation. The priest was a mere medium, his function limited to the purveyance of bread and wine. Chief always attended the Communion services, and when she spoke to us about them, shortly before we were confirmed, she gave us to understand that the main virtue of the mystic bread and wine was to give us the strength and reinforcement of our will in our fight against the world, the flesh and the devil.

*   *   *

In nomine ...

It is Sunday evening, about six o'clock. Outside, in the deserted park, the swathes of fine rain-mist roll up towards the house, trailing between naked trees and erasing the fine-drawn line of the little stream, which emerges to sight only near the house, like a black ribbon in soft grey hair. In the harsh light of unshaded electric bulbs, we get out our hymn-books, for the chapel bell is ringing. We are stiff with cold. The fires are dying down and the vast rooms with their torn tapestry wall-papers are raw and chilly. The gilt mirrors are glazed with children's breath. In silence we walk down stone passages, past the kitchens with their warm, sickly odours and the raucous sound of servants' voices. For them, perhaps, a hot supper amid a smell of dish-cloths, but for us, plates of bread and butter and bowls of jelly, the Sunday evening treat. As we go into chapel, the harmonium is wheezing out the slow movement from Beethoven's 'Pathétique' sonata. The candles are lit on the altar, the chapel half-full of children, some sitting with their blue serge coats drawn closely over their shoulders, others at their conventional, pre-service prayers. I, a member of the choir, await service in the vestry behind heavy baize curtains, smelling of dust and tallow. The harmonium pants on its way, like the hart in the psalm. The organist has started the movement again, for, as always, Chief is late. We stand in silence, shifting from one cold foot to the other. We never talk or whisper or play about. We have been made to feel that it is our chapel, that our God inhabits it, only waiting to be released from His habitual silence and reserve by the prayers the Head will pray on our behalf. Then a pad, pad in the passage outside, the click of the latch on the chapel door, a hand swings back the vestry curtain with infinite grace, and Chief is before us, resplendent in mortar-board, gown and royal blue hood. We bow our heads.

'Lord, let the words of our mouths and the meditation of our hearts be always acceptable in Thy sight.'

Chief speaks in a low voice for our ears alone. We are the elect. For us the especial prayer, the private moment with God. Then we start our procession up the chapel and the chairs scrape as the children rise to their feet at our passing and watch us as we stalk, stiff and majestic, to our places in the chancel. We pray. We rise. Chief takes the paper from her prayer-desk and reads out the number of the opening hymn. On the asbestos roof of the chapel the rain beats incessantly a monotonous and dismal accompaniment to our childish orisons.

At last the lessons are over, the canticles and the collects. We relax on to our chairs, the chill of the evening enveloping us, anaesthetizing us, the altar candles guttering in the draught which always sweeps through the chancel from the side door. It is time for the address. Her mortar-board left behind by her chair, Chief steps up to the pulpit. She smiles a little, as if she had God by the hand and were introducing Him to us, and speaks:

'I want to remind you tonight of words we all too easily forget, words which our Lord and Saviour spoke to His disciples, before they set out on their pilgrimage. He knew how hard the way would be. He knew that this weary wicked world of ours is no place for weaklings, for doubters, for cowards. Yet He knew, too, that these twelve men He had chosen – these twelve who are in some ways so like us – would often be weak, would long to give up the struggle, would turn back over and over again from the straight path. And so He spoke to them of the work He wanted them to do, not once but many times; He warned them of tribulation and persecution; He tried to give them His own strength, His own endurance, His own steadfastness of purpose in their coming struggle.

' "If any man will come after me, let him deny himself, and take up his cross daily, and follow me."

'Daily – that is the word He stresses. That is the word we have to remember. He never allowed those friends of His to sit back, to slack and sloom as we do. It was a hard life they led with Him. He didn't spare them, nor did He spare Himself.

'What were these men like, who walked the hills of Galilee with our Lord, through burning wind and sun and winter rain? They were physically strong men, fishermen, many of them, used to enduring long hours in wind and weather, yet our Lord knew that the world, the flesh and the devil are stronger than wind and rain, and that they could not overcome the world without His help. Ruthlessly, He trained their minds and bodies.

' "Take nothing for your journey, neither staves, nor scrip, neither bread, neither money..."

'He said. He warned them clearly of what was to come:

' "Beware of men: for they will deliver you up
to the councils, and they will scourge you
in their synagogues."

'And so He warns us. He tells us plainly that our way is
not easy. He urges us to train ourselves like those early disciples. I want you to understand Gud's purposes. When you
are faced with difficulties, when the ways of the world seem
hard and unjust, when this school in which you live – this
school to which you belong and which belongs to you –
seems a harsh place, a place of few soft comforts, a place of
discipline and rigour – I want you to remember that Gud
has placed you here for a purpose, and given you these
opportunities of training yourselves for that very purpose.
I want you to remember the words of Jesus to His disciples:

' "If any man will come after Me, let him deny
himself and take up his cross daily and follow Me."

'Above all, I want you to remember Christ's own example,
that example which the fortunate disciples had always before
their very eyes. I want you to see Christ as they saw Him.
That is the Gud I want you to worship. Not the remote,
bearded Father in heaven. Not the meek and mild young
man of the Bible pictures. But the Gud who came down to
earth, Who sweated over a carpenter's bench, the Gud Who
sat in the stern of a boat and talked with fishermen, the
Gud Who turned the money-changers out of the temple,
and the Gud Who, finally, hanging on a cross, cried to His
companions, two robbers, "Today shalt thou be with Me
in Paradise."

'What are *we* like? We give way at the smallest pain, the
slightest difficulty. We slack and sloom through life, doing

the least we can, turning aside from every trial, every danger. How should we behave if we were tortured and persecuted as He was? We, who cannot even put up with a headache, or a disappointment? In this weary world of ours we shall have to face many hard and bitter things. We need His courage. We need His pride. Above all we need His will. That is what is the matter with us all today. Lack of will-power, lack of self-control. We know what is right and wrong. Gud has put into our hearts a conscience. We've all got one, whether we like it or not, and it tells us, however hard we shut our ears to it, it tells us what is right and what is wrong, what is the brave thing to do and what is the cowardly thing. Why? Because our wills are not equal to the demands of our consciences. Because we lack the self-control to reject the easy wrong and choose the difficult right. We think we can get away with shoddy work, with slack, easy lives, with selfishness and greed and indifference. But we can't, you know. Every time we do the easy, worth-less thing, instead of the hard, worth-while thing, we lose a little more of our will-power and self-control, until we are no longer capable of exerting it. When that time comes we are worthless – worthless to Gud and man. It is up to us, each one of us, every day and every hour of the day, to exert this power within us, to practise control over ourselves, so that we can, with Gud's grace, conquer the world, the flesh and the devil, as He did. He never faltered. He was brave to the end. He could subdue His own sufferings so far that He could forgive His enemies, even on the Cross, and comfort the suffering sinners on either side of Him. That is a Gud worth having. That is a Gud worth following. That is a Gud worth worshipping. I am going to end this address with words that you may have heard me quote before:

‘ "I'll not bow
To the gentle Jesus of the women, I –
But to the man who hung 'twixt earth and heaven
Six mortal hours, and knew the end (as strength
And custom was) three days away, yet ruled
His soul and body so, that when the sponge
Blessed His cracked lips with promise of relief
And quick oblivion, He would not drink:
He turned His head away and would not drink:
Spat out the anodyne and would not drink.
This was a god for kings and queens of pride,
And Him I follow."

‘ "And now to Gud the Father, Gud the Son, and Gud
the Holy Ghost, be all honour..." '

As I rise to my feet I am writing hurriedly on the back of
my hymn-book Sunday's date and the words: 'Elizabeth's
speech, from *Will Shakespeare* by Clemence Dane.' When
chapel is over I shall compare notes with my friends. We
keep a scrupulous score of the Head's quotations, and at
present I have a lead of three points.

*   *   *

Although Chief's attitude to religion was undoctrinal, she
realized that we could hardly be confirmed without some
professional preparation, and she allowed old Canon Naylor
or his even older brother, to take confirmation classes. Once
I had made up my mind to attend them, I looked forward
to them keenly, for I was prepared to be deeply interested
in my religion. Alas, though my interest remained, my
belief was short-lived.

I was dismayed by Canon Naylor's animadversions on the Catechism, through which he took us laboriously, line by line. It appeared that this was Holy Writ, and every word in it pregnant with meaning. While we pored over the significance of 'What is your name? N or M.', confirmation gradually receded from sight till it became as remote as the Last Judgment. Having successfully banished all reality from the ceremony, Canon Naylor would then speak of it with bated breath, in the same manner as he spoke of the descent of the dove at the Baptism of Jesus, or the Immaculate Conception (which, for all his glosses, I never understood). Confirmation became so mysterious a rite that I could hardly conceive of my mundane self taking part in it and still living. I became as breathless as Canon Naylor. At the fittings of my confirmation dress, I was filled with as much mystic adoration as if I were donning the habit of a nun. I used to go to chapel by myself and say prayers of such mystical rarity that I cannot believe that they ever reached the Deity but must have wandered about, like wisps of smoke, in the *Ewigkeit.*

Confirmation day brought me my first major disillusionment. There was no mystery, no descent of a dove, no flooding of the soul with heavenly radiance. A stout, elderly man, in gorgeous clothes, laid a soft hand like a bag of feathers on my head, and that was all. I rose from the chancel steps, and with seven or eight other initiates, white-garbed, veiled and blushing, walked down the aisle to the candidates' reserved pew. I was aware then, as I had not been aware before the laying on of hands, of the gaping crowd who had come to witness the ceremony. There were rows of children in their dark gym tunics. All wore hats for this occasion, in deference to the Bishop whose presence was able, as God's apparently was not, to bestow consecration upon the chapel. Under the heavily brimmed hats their pink, curious faces looked up at me as I walked slowly down the aisle in my hideous white frock and black stockings. What were they thinking? I suppose they were looking, as I had looked inwardly, for some outer evidence of change. They, like me, were disappointed. I was not transfigured. There was no unearthly light around my drooping head and no stigmata on my hot, clasped hands. I was just Rachel Curgenven – hot, uncomfortable and embarrassed, longing to get out of these clothes into my gym tunic again.

The following Sunday we took our first Communion. For this we had also been prepared by Canon Naylor. He had dealt with the service faithfully in the same manner as he had dealt with the Catechism. Every sentence, every word almost, was dwelt upon. Each had its gloss, and by the time he had finished with it, the naked simplicity, the bare bones of it, had been draped in flowery interpretations. I remember his long dissertation upon the words 'We do not *presume* to come to Thy table.' This was intended to be a text for humility, but I do not think Canon Naylor understood the nature of humility. He told us that we did not *presume* to come to God's table simply because we had nothing of worth in us, no gifts, no virtues, however small; because we were worms. It was not therefore a matter of humility, to my mind, but of cringing beggary. In utter destitution we were to approach that table and pick up the crumbs. We were the recipients of God's condescension. This view of the Eucharist was repugnant to me.

Yet despite the tedious doctrinal teaching of Canon Naylor, despite the profound disappointment that I was not translated at my confirmation, I was ardently desirous of taking my first Communion, and believed that here at last I would by-pass the foolishness of men and make direct contact with the divine presence. I had always been critical and sceptical. I had even ridiculed much of what I heard in school prayers, and chapel, but fundamentally I wanted to believe. I went to my first Communion in a dedicated frame of mind.

I emerged feeling utterly cheated, swindled, defrauded. Maybe I had expected too much – that I accepted and felt to be my own fault. But I had thought that God had a part to play as well. After all, it was I who was in darkness. I could only reach out my hands, and that I had done. There was nothing there. Any competent priest could have torn this to pieces in five minutes, but not to my spiritual satisfaction. The priest had an answer to everything, but I had never wanted the answers at second-hand. I wanted them at first-hand – doubtless a sin of spiritual pride – and when at the age of sixteen I had stumbled on the emptiness that lies beyond our five senses, I was not prepared to fill it either with what others told me must be there, or with my own imagination. I accepted the emptiness for what it was and I have found it impossible to believe in God since.

CHAPTER FOURTEEN

Fortunatus et ille deos qui novit agrestis.
Panaque Silvanumque senem Nymphasque sorores.
VIRGIL

*(Fortunate that man who knows his country gods, Pan and old Silvanus and the sister
spirits of the woods.)*

THE May term came, and Rachel felt the acute restlessness
of the young animal in springtime. Unable in this nunnery
to find any normal outlet for her emotions, she sought
violent physical exercise. All over the park, trees had been
felled that winter, and left lying, to be carried into the wood
sheds in the early summer, sawn up and stacked for the
following autumn.

'Chief,' said Rachel, one morning, catching Miss Faulkner
as she came out of assembly, 'Chief, I want to do some work
in the park.'

Chief slipped her arm over Rachel's shoulders and
propelled her gently down the passage towards the
front hall. They paused in front of a huge bowl of red
tulips.

'Wonderful,' said Chief, appreciatively, and caressed one
of the pear-shaped flowers with her smooth hands. 'Wonderful. Now, come along, my dear Curgenven, we'll take a
walk in the park, and you can tell me what it is you want
to do.'

They walked slowly across the deserted cricket pitches.

'It's the wood-sawing, and the collecting up of the felled

trees,' said Rachel, at last. 'I wondered if you'd let me help the men. I like sawing.'

'Do you? Can you use a saw? Or an axe?'

'I've used one at home.'

'Let's walk round to the wood sheds and talk to Tarrant.'

The white house shimmered softly in the heat; the great elms, grouped at one end of the playing fields, smoked in the sun in the humid atmosphere. A little way off the deer were grazing, and Chief's words were punctuated by their staccato coughs. A pleasant sense of well-being, bred of this flattering intimacy and the soft charm of the scene, came over Rachel, and the weight of Chief's arm upon her own seemed an honourable burden.

Slowly they walked round, past the Big Hall, past the chapel, past the concrete on which punishment drill took place. In the wood sheds, Tarrant and another man were unloading tree trunks from the cart and stacking them. There was a sweet smell of sawdust.

'I've brought you a second mate, Tarrant,' said Chief. She got on well with the men of the estate. She had the hereditary gift of dealing with servants, of managing estates, of judging horses and trees and soil. The men touched their caps, and Tarrant looked Rachel up and down.

'Meaning the young lady, ma'am?' he asked in his broad Somerset voice.

'Yes, let her come and work here. Watch her with an axe, Tarrant. If she can use it properly, she has my permission to come whenever she likes.'

'Right, ma'am.' Nothing surprised the Bampfield men. 'Are you starting now, Miss Rachel?'

'Well, I ought to be doing French, I believe,' said Rachel guiltily.

'Go ahead,' said Chief, increasing the pressure of her arm a little before withdrawing it. 'Go ahead. It's not one of your University Entrance subjects. You can say you had my permission to miss it.'

Chief was a woman accustomed to cutting through ordinary routine, to brushing aside convention and habit as often as she created it. At that moment, Rachel could have knelt down and kissed her hand. She waited till Chief had gone and then rolled up her sleeves. The men took her advent as a matter of course. It was thus, by an unexpected act of understanding, that Chief bound to her devotion those spirits like Rachel, whose bent led them towards imaginative fields. At another school, no such permission would have been given, no such work, probably, would have been available. Swinging an axe in the warm, moted sunshine of the woodyard restored Rachel to her sense of proportion. And there were hours of even greater delight, when she would escape from games or prep, and find Tarrant just lifting the last tree from the cart. He would let her take the horse out into the park, with his assistant, a silent, red-faced Somersetshire boy called Jeff, too overcome by the proximity of a young lady to speak a single word, except unintelligible syllables to the aged horse. They would plod solemnly over the soft grass towards the fallen trees. Together they would lift the branches into the cart. Jeff, with perspiring chivalry, always endeavoured to do the main work of heaving up the trunks. Purple with exertion, his hairy arms running with sweat, he grunted and occasionally uttered strange, animal noises that Rachel took to be oaths, and she vied with him in her exertions, till it became almost a contest between them as to which should get the heaviest end of the tree into the cart.

She would return from these expeditions, or from the wood-cutting in the yard, a different person, would sit in the prefects' room, working at an essay, impervious to the gossip and by-play around her. She would stand in Georgie's room, sunburnt and assured, unaware of the impression of vitality she created, murmuring dangerous badinage and talking with a familiarity the effect of which she little understood.

The outdoor work brought her into contact, too, with Punch. As Rachel was not in her house, and had dropped Geography, which was Punch's chief subject, her contacts with this Bampfield eccentric were few. But Punch was responsible for some of the outdoor organization of the place, and Rachel found great pleasure in some of the odd scraps of conversation they indulged in, when they met at the wood sheds, or walked up the long lime avenue together to the market gardens. More and more, the staff tended to treat Rachel almost as an adult, and Punch would discuss with her the latest biography she had read, or retail for her amusement some strange piece of information she had culled from an obscure journal, or an old book. She was earthy and outspoken, and endlessly curious, and succeeded in destroying some of Rachel's primness.

Of Miss Burnett, Rachel saw a great deal. Their relations were not always easy. But there were periods when Miss Burnett was moody and irritable; when a feverish look appeared in her eye and a bitter twist to her mouth. On one occasion, they were translating Catullus – '*Odi et amo.*' Miss Burnett read the words slowly in Latin, lingeringly drawling their syllables. 'Go on,' she said, 'translate it.'

'I hate and I love,' began Rachel.

'Oh, leave out that feeble "and",' said Miss Burnett.

' "Et" in Latin has a hundred times the force of "and" in English.'

'Shall I strengthen it with a "yet"?' suggested Rachel. 'I hate and yet I love?' Her versifying instinct told her that this sounded more melodious.

'No,' snarled Miss Burnett. 'Leave it out. If you cannot find an equivalent word, be forceful by omission. "I hate ... I love".'

Disturbed at the vicious tone of her voice, Rachel ploughed her way solemnly through the second line. There was a moment's silence.

'Oh, God,' groaned Miss Burnett, 'that I am condemned to teach schoolgirls.' She rose abruptly, went to the window and lit a cigarette. Turning so that her golden hair appeared like an aureole round her dark, bitter face, and the smoke from her lips suffusing the whole window, she said, 'How can you possibly understand those words? Go away. Go and play your silly games in the prefects' room.'

Bitterly hurt, Rachel swept up her books and left the room. Hardly knowing where she was going, she found herself running down the lime avenue towards the stables, without even bothering to see if anyone was watching her or following. All the months of spring the garden had remained in her mind; why had she never visited it since that February night? She could not have answered; its magical quality had been its own invisible protection, perhaps, making a further visit – a visit of curiosity – a violation. But now she was in desperate need of it.

She had no pliers, but the wire where she had last entered the shrubbery was very insecurely fastened and yielded easily to her fingers. Still clasping her Catullus, she stumbled through the undergrowth. Her hands were green as she pushed the branches aside, and then, as she came out into the clearing, she saw before her the silent, weeded lake, the pagoda, bright amid the trees, the little bridges, the tiny peninsula with its rotting boathouse still miraculously faultless, its timbers precariously supporting the carved roof.

She still had not told Margaret that she had found the garden. She shut out from her mind the fact that Margaret knew of it, preferring to imagine it her own domain. It sprang to her mind, in absence, as a complete image, precise in detail. Reason told her that the ponds were no longer clear, but thick with silt and fallen leaves. But it never occurred to her to deplore its decay. She accepted the place as she accepted a poem. It imaged for her an inner order behind chaotic and unlovely everyday existence. It reflected the logic of that other world, and it held within its narrow rim a draught of pure poetry. It was a thing created for delight, no matter how artificial a conception, or how decayed by time. It was subject to spirits, to arcane gods, whose presence she never recognized consciously, but whose influence she felt, benign and revealing. From then on, she went to the garden over and over again. Though any meaning attached to her visits was only dimly apprehended, it was sufficiently within her reach to induce her to pursue it, as she pursued the meaning of a poem, say one by Thomas the Rhymer, and as with that poem one enters a little deeper into its meaning with every reading, so she entered more deeply into the world of the Chinese garden every time she visited it.

This term had brought an important change to Rachel and one which had considerable bearing on her happiness. She was made a prefect. This diverted her restless, domineering side (described in school reports as a gift for leadership) into more legitimate channels.

The appointment as prefect coincided with a period of intellectual pleasure which balanced the physical delights of the park and woodyard. It was, therefore, a period of equilibrium, one which rarely offers itself to any personality, and it brought Rachel the last measure of content which Bampfield was to afford her. Just as her flowering physical strength had found an immediate outlet in her work with the tree-fellers, so her growing intellectual powers found plentiful material to work on in the fields of literature which were opening up before her. Rachel's English work was now entirely done in private coaching with a member of the staff with whom she had previously had little contact. This was Miss Naylor.

Miss Naylor was stone deaf and precluded from class teaching by this disability. She did only coaching work and secretarial chores for Chief. She lived in a small world of her own, seemingly armed against Bampfield's rigours and eccentricities by her inner philosophic content: *Teres atque rotundus*, like Horace's happy man, and smoothed and rounded in her own person too – a kind of human Mrs Tiggy-Winkle in appearance. If her deafness was a barrier, it was also a protection. Perhaps also it affected her olfactory sense, for her ill-furnished room smelt overpoweringly of cat and cat's fish. She had two tabby beasts and kept for them an earth-box which never appeared to have been emptied when I saw it, while saucers of stale fish and dusty milk were arranged in one corner. The room was full of books, good, solid, old-fashioned editions of the poets and novelists, books which at most had been names to me, and which opened up a very different world from that of Chief's favourite poets – Masefield, Noyes and Kipling. I remember well when I first heard these words from Coleridge's *Christabel*, read to me in Miss Naylor's even voice:

> Is the night chilly and dark?
> The night is chilly, but not dark.
> The thin gray cloud is spread on high,
> It covers but not hides the sky.
> The moon is behind, and at the full;
> And yet she looks both small and dull.
> The night is chill, the cloud is gray:
> 'Tis a month before the month of May,
> And the Spring comes slowly up this way.

The whole room – cats, earth-box, books and all – dissolved into a sheeted moonlight, and I felt at my heart the spell of evil that haunts the poem, and that lurked in the reedy park of Bampfield itself.

For my University Entrance, I studied the Romantics. Shut off from the everyday world by her deafness, Miss Naylor seemed to have slipped into and to belong to the world of *Lamia* and *Isabella*, and *The Corsair*. As she read, her eye and voice had much the same compelling power over me as Coleridge's *Ancient Mariner*. She gave me the impression of having participated in the writing of the poems herself, so complete was her identification.

She opened my eyes not only to the Romantics but to the Moderns and for this I am profoundly grateful to her. They did not enter into my syllabus, but one day she produced a newly published book of modern verse. She did not read a great deal with me – she was too wise for that – but in the two or three poems that she did read, she succeeded in conveying to me her own delight in the discovery of these, as they then seemed, outlandish poets. I can hear her now, reading E. E. Cummings with enormous gusto and relish:

                (the
          Flics, tidiyum, are
          very tidiyum reassuringly similar,
          they all have very tidiyum
          mustaches, and very
          tidiyum chins, and just above
          their very tidiyum ears their
          very tidiyum necks begin)

And a phrase from another poet – I have forgotten who – still sticks in my mind:

          Or a great cloud entering the room of the sky,
          Napoleon of his century,
          Heard come to knowing music consciously.

And, of course, there was Eliot's *The Waste Land*, which I hardly understood, but found myself returning to over and over again. It was at least ten years before I bought myself a copy of that anthology. The barren years at the University and the still more barren struggle to earn a living, destroyed temporarily my desire for poetry, but I came back to it in the end, and when I reread those poems, I could hear Miss Naylor's keen, humorous and appreciative tones, and I picked up, as an adult, my old enthusiasms and carried them forward.

The balanced life of authority, physical work and intellectual discovery was at least temporarily so satisfying that Rachel hardly felt her isolation from her fellows. But to Bisto the position was intolerable. Cut off from Rachel, her worried face assumed an air of perpetual and unassuageable grief. Bampfield, which she had always hated, now held for her the horrors of a concentration camp. Her work, never brilliant, became almost moronic, and her behaviour so erratic and absent-minded that she was perpetually in the hands of Miss Christian Lucas. Bisto was, however, at least in Rachel's house. It was still possible to speak to her during the informal house dance every Friday night. She could see Rachel when she was on 'lights' duty as a prefect and had to parade the dormitories. If it was no more than a few words she spoke, they were a comfort to the unhappy Bisto.

'How's Willy?' asked Rachel one night, idly. Bisto's eyes filled.

'I haven't seen him for ages. I expect he's dead,' she replied. 'I don't like going down to the stables by myself.'

Rachel switched off the light abruptly and closed the door. It was not possible to discuss the matter. Out in the darkened passage she paused for a moment, thinking of afternoons spent with Bisto in the stables; hours in the secret paths with Margaret, smoking and talking; long walks outside the park during the previous autumn when they raided orchards and lay against warm ricks, munching stolen fruit. It all seemed very far away. Of Margaret Rachel saw nothing now. She was in another house and their paths seldom crossed. But Rachel began to notice that the grass at the spot where Margaret entered the shrubbery was well trodden down. It looked as if she had been there a good many times this term, and she wondered a little that their visits had never coincided.

One fine morning in June, when the sun was drawing up a pale vapour from the marshy park, Rachel came away from her coaching with Miss Naylor, carrying Coleridge's poems under her arm, and 'Xanadu' in her head.

'Where Alph the sacred river ran ...' she repeated to herself, and the words brought to her mind the stream running through the Chinese garden. The broken pagoda glittered again with gilt and colour and copper bells, and the ornamental bridges glowed between the ferns and berberis.

'I must go there this afternoon,' she thought, and absented herself from games, ostensibly to go for a walk.

There was no one about. With a distaste for Margaret's well-worn track, she entered the shrubbery from almost the opposite side. She undid the wire, pulled out a paling and began to force her way through the cool, damp undergrowth. There was no path, of course, and amid new-growing brambles and pithy elders, she lost her way. At one moment she paused and heard in the silence the faint trickle of water. 'Alph, the sacred river,' she murmured and turned towards it. She came out of the undergrowth on the side of the lake where the river carried its water out towards the fence again. Some confused memory of Greek tradition mingled with *Kubla Khan* in her mind, and she stooped on the bank of the stream and scooped some of the water up into her hands. She wetted her forehead, drank a sip of the water, and poured the rest out ceremoniously on the ground, as a libation to the gods of the place.

She was astonished and moved by the powerful effect of this sudden emergence upon the well-known scene. Her mind full of 'Xanadu', she felt her armour drop from her and knew herself willingly vulnerable to the assault of this strange world where poetry was 'felt in the blood and felt along the heart'. She lay down in the long grass at the side of the pool. A little above her, if she inclined her head, she could see the drooping eaves of the pagoda. There was the bridge, and beyond it the green surface of the second pool, with its weeping willow and boathouse. There was no wind. Birds were busy in the trees and bushes. The scent of earth, broken by rising shoots, the warm aromatic smell of the berberis, the vivid, incongruous carving of the bridges, set down amid quiet elders and moss, all were caught up in a web of poetry. The garden seemed to hang in mid-air like Coleridge's sunny dome. In this compelling reality, Bampfield seemed no more than a dream.

She began to read, turning over the pages of the complete Coleridge she had brought—*Kubla Khan, Frost at Midnight, This Lime-tree Bower my Prison*, and then ... *Christabel*:

' And in my dream methought I went
To search out what might there be found;
And what the sweet bird's trouble meant,
That thus lay fluttering on the ground.
I went and peered, and could descry
No cause for her distressful cry;
But yet for her dear lady's sake
I stooped methought the dove to take...'

She heard the sound of branches being pushed aside and looked up to see Margaret emerging from the undergrowth near her. No thought of their school relationship entered her mind. Margaret was caught up as easily as *Christabel*, and with hardly a greeting to her she went on reading, as though both had a right to the garden. It was Margaret who was disconcerted. She stared at Rachel, and after a moment came up to her and looked over her shoulder.

' "When lo! I saw a bright green snake
Coiled around its wings and neck.

127

Green as the herbs on which it couched,
Close by the dove's its head it crouched;
And with the dove it heaves and stirs,
Swelling its neck as she swelled hers!
I woke; it was the midnight hour,
The clock was echoing in the tower;
But though my slumber was gone by,
This dream it would not pass away –
It seems to live upon my eye!" '

Margaret was reading the words aloud, and she added, 'I didn't know you came here. I suppose Chief's given you the key?' She sounded annoyed.

'No, I get in like you do. Through the fence.'

Margaret's eyes brightened. 'But – you're a prefect!'

'It doesn't count here. Forget it.'

'I won't say anything.' There was an urgency in Margaret's voice.

'It never occurred to me that you would.'

'Rachel, do read me some more of that poem.'

'Don't you know it?' asked Rachel.

'I don't think so,' said Margaret, sitting down beside her on the moss. 'At any rate, I don't recognize that bit. Read it to me.'

'It's rather long,' answered Rachel. 'I don't mind reading a part of it, though.'

She began near the end, reading the verses which describe Bracy's dream.

' "A snake's small eye blinks dull and shy;
And the lady's eyes they shrunk in her head,
Each shrunk up to a serpent's eye,

And with somewhat of malice, but more
      of dread,
At Christabel she looked askance! –
One moment – and the sight was fled!
But Christabel in dizzy trance
Stumbling on the unsteady ground
Shuddered aloud, with a hissing sound;
And Geraldine again turned round,
And like a thing that sought relief,
Full of wonder and full of grief,
She rolled her large bright eyes divine
Wildly on Sir Leoline." '

Absorbed, Rachel read on, unaware of Margaret's face, so
close beside her own. She shut the book, and looked up.
'There, that's all. He never finished it.'
   'It could have happened here, couldn't it?' said Margaret.
'If the pagoda were a castle? One can imagine it. I found a
grass snake here in the autumn, just like the one in the
poem. Why do they look so evil? They're beautiful, yet
they're evil.'
Margaret was pulling up the moss in tufts as she spoke,
and filling one palm with the green feathers. Clenched in her
hand, they looked like the tousled body of a dead green
bird.
   'Rachel, tell me why the most beautiful things are often
evil?'
   'I don't know that they are.'
   'I do.'
   'This garden isn't. It's perfect, in a ruined, desolate way.
I can't see that it's evil.'
   'Yet I found a snake in it,' said Margaret.

'A snake isn't really evil.'

'It's a symbol of evil. And it's an omen. You'll see. They'll find us out and then they'll tear back the fence and admit evil – they'll turn it all into something foul.'

Rachel did not know what to reply to this. She had never thought very seriously about the problem of evil. Indeed, her rebellious atheism, propped up by classical reading, inclined her to regard evil as a creation of the Church.

'Where did you find the snake?' she asked, her curiosity aroused. 'He ought to be awake now. I'd love to see him.'

'He was near the pagoda,' answered Margaret. 'He probably went to sleep under the floorboards for warmth.'

'Let's go and look,' said Rachel, and they climbed the rotting wooden steps up to the little building.

'Perhaps if he hears our footsteps he'll come out.'

Rachel made a noise with her feet, and the two girls walked slowly round the pagoda, tapping the wooden sides and knocking the floor softly. But no snake appeared.

'Perhaps,' said Margaret, 'it's a she-snake and once was a kind of Christabel. She lived at Bampfield and used to come here to meet her lover and then as they swooned in each other's arms in ecstasy, she dropped down to the floor, a snake, and glided away into the undergrowth.'

'Why should she?' asked Rachel, in whom the stream of poetry set flowing by Christabel was now only trickling slowly. 'Why on earth should she?'

'Because,' said Margaret slowly, 'her love was evil in the eyes of the world.'

Rachel looked at her watch. 'Oh, lord, it's time I was getting back.'

'Rachel, will you come again?'

'I expect so,' said Rachel warily. She did not wish to commit herself to clandestine meetings with Margaret.

'Can I meet you here?'

Yes, she might have known Margaret would extract that. Rachel moved awkwardly away from her, aware suddenly of the intrusion of school into this enchanted place.

'I'd rather not.'

'Oh, God, you are stuffy!' cried Margaret angrily, and Rachel felt ashamed and hurt. 'As if I'd tell anyone we met. I never see you. You are the only person in this lousy hole that I can talk to, that can talk intelligently.'

'Well, if you go on coming here,' said Rachel, 'I suppose we're bound to meet.'

'Please meet me, next week at this time.'

'Why are you here, anyway?' asked Rachel, suspiciously, the prefect in her rising up.

'Oh, I got out of games,' said Margaret evasively.

'I must go,' said Rachel. Something was threatening the garden. She was no longer at ease there. It became an urgent matter to get out.

'Look, we can't be seen going back together. You go first,' she said to Margaret, 'otherwise you'll be late for something.'

Margaret disappeared down the path and Rachel turned her back on her and looked across the green lake. At one corner stood the derelict boathouse and a shallow boat still lay within it, embedded in mud. She had never explored it. She walked slowly over to it, wondering if the boat could by any chance be floated again. When she reached it, she was surprised to see that it was quite clean inside, and that some-one had made a bed of dried fern in the bottom of it. But it would never be floated, she thought. The planks were rotten and one side broken down almost to the duckboards. If the water had not drained away to the lake, leaving it much shallower than its original state, the boat would have been under water. For a moment, Rachel stood looking down at it, wondering at the dried ferns. Then she packed up her books into a leather case and made her way to the fence.

That evening was the weekly house dance. As always, Bisto claimed Rachel for a number. It was the high spot of the week for her, the only moment when she could talk to Rachel and forget that she was a prefect.

'Margaret cut games today,' she began conversationally, as they waltzed slowly round the room, while the pianist thumped out 'When you and I were Seventeen'.

'Yes,' said Rachel, without thinking.

'Did you know?' asked Bisto quickly.

Rachel recovered herself. 'I heard the others talking about it. Did she get into a row?'

'She's got P.D. for it tomorrow.'

'Poor devil!'

'I've got it too,' said Bisto miserably.

Rachel looked down at her, moved for a moment with sympathy and some of her old tenderness for the faithful, anxious creature.

'*You've* got it? Oh, lord, Bisto, I suppose Christian will take it out on you.'

'I suppose so. And you won't be there. It wasn't so bad when you were there too, or at least free to meet me afterwards.'

'Ah, that's one of the blessings of being a prefect. No P.D.'

'Do you enjoy being a prefect?'

Rachel felt slightly uncomfortable. Bisto was too much

like her conscience. She *did* enjoy being a prefect. Alas, she enjoyed all the wrong things. The dance came to an end, and Rachel went off to dance with a fellow prefect, thoughtful and a little depressed, remembering with regret the old days of feeding Willy in the stables, strolling in the shrubbery paths, and smoking in the corn bins in the evening.

CHAPTER FIFTEEN

———————

The summer is ended and we are not saved.
JEREMIAH

RACHEL was beginning to be conscious of a split which ran right across her world, like a brown crack in a plate. The garden now became more and more a necessity to her and she visited it almost with a sense of urgency, as though any message it had for her must be sought now or lost for ever. The garden itself was changed. It was very lush, and overgrown with new shoots. There hung over it a rich, rather sickly smell that came from the many fungi growing in the mossy earth, and between the cracks in the boards of the pagoda and bridges. Something of the corruption of Bampfield itself had soaked down into the red earth and was drawn up again in the vapours which wrapped the shrubbery in the early morning and evening during that hot, damp July, as though veiling it from the world's eyes for some secret and appalling rite.

One afternoon, when Rachel was standing near the boat-house, she noticed that the stern timbers had fallen off the punt, and someone – Margaret presumably – had stacked them neatly against the boat's side. The fern in the bottom had been recently renewed. After a moment's hesitation, she stepped in and lay down on it, propping herself on one elbow to read.

She found it difficult to give her attention to the page. The garden was full of sounds, and her heightened sensibilities

134

were alive to each one. She stirred restlessly, and for the first time since she had come there, felt herself afraid of intrusion. She had deliberately avoided meeting Margaret again, and assumed that she, like herself, had taken the trouble to find out times when it was impossible for them to meet. Ill at ease, she felt compelled at last to leave the boathouse.

It was then that she saw Margaret sitting on the steps of the pagoda.

'I've been watching you for some time,' said Margaret.

'Why didn't you say something?'

'You were reading. I didn't want to interrupt. The boat's comfortable, isn't it?'

'Very. I suppose you often lie in it.'

'Not often. But sometimes. We haven't met for ages, Rachel. Have you tried to avoid me?'

Rachel said nothing.

'I want to talk to you badly sometimes. And this is the only place one can escape to.'

Helplessly, Rachel saw the indefinable magic of the garden being reduced to the mere status of an escape from school. Was it no more than this to Margaret?

'Have you read this yet?' asked Margaret suddenly, and held out a book. Rachel looked at the title. It was Radclyffe Hall's *The Well of Loneliness*.

'No,' she said. 'I haven't.'

'I've nearly finished it. I bought it in the holidays. I keep it in the pagoda, in a box.'

A series of images began slowly to draw together in a pattern, incomprehensible as yet – the fern-strewn boat, the book in the pagoda, the picture of Cleopatra, the green snake.

'Will you read it if I leave it here?'

'I don't know,' said Rachel.

'You ought to read it. It's a marvellous book.'

'It's getting near the end of the term. I've a lot of reading to do. I don't think I'll have time.'

'Well, I'll leave it there,' said Margaret. 'Please read it.'

'I can't promise,' said Rachel uncomfortably. 'I've got such a hell of a lot to do.'

She rose, anxious to prevent Margaret from saying anything further. When she looked back from the edge of the pool, Margaret was walking slowly over towards the boathouse, reading as she went.

Rachel did not go to the garden again that summer term. She threw herself into her work and her prefect's duties with immense energy. She tried to see Bisto whenever she could, for it was her last term. She was leaving early to finish her education abroad. Rachel realized with a pang that she was going to miss her. So many of her contemporaries were going either that term or next. She herself would shortly be a house captain, and most of the prefects would be younger than her. There was the staff, of course, with some of whom, by virtue of her age and her special university work, she was on fairly intimate terms, but there were few that she liked really well.

The prospect of eight weeks away from Bampfield endeared the place to her, and brought her back on to old, familiar terms with it. She made two or three surreptitious expeditions with Bisto to various haunts, especially to Willy, who was left enough food (at the expense of almost a total dinner) to last him, it was hoped, for at least three weeks.

'Then he will have to fend for himself,' said Bisto sorrowfully.

'We must all learn to be independent,' said Rachel. 'Even rats.' And, feeling more like her old self, she adopted Chief's manner and continued: 'Gud has put into our hands – into our paws – the priceless power to make our own way in this weary wicked world of ours. Gud will help us if we ask Him, but – do we want to ask Him? A thousand times, no! Rats, let us stand on our own four feet – paws – and battle our way on, secure in the knowledge that underneath are the everlasting paws, and recognizing bravely that our weakness is His strength – or the other way round, I really can't remember.

> ' "Make strong in me a heart too brave
> To ask Thee anything."

'D'you hear that, Willy?' And Bisto joining in with her, the two girls chanted to the wondering rat:

> ' "Make strong in me a heart too brave
> To ask Thee anything." '

'Oh, he is greedy,' cried Bisto ruefully. 'He's taken the bit of meat now that was intended to be saved up for the feast at the end. And I tucked it right away at the bottom of the pile.'

'Trust Willy,' said Rachel. 'He knows when he's on to a good thing. No Bampfield self-control for him. I don't suppose Gud will mind. He probably has a different law for rats.'

It was a melancholy end of term. Being the summer, there were no special religious festivities, nothing to shed a ritual light over the breaking-up, only Chief's voice intoning mellifluously the usual end of term lesson:

' "Cast thy bread upon the waters: for thou shalt find it after many days. Give a portion to seven, and also to eight." '

Bisto heard it with tears in her eyes. It reminded her of Willy. Hateful though Bampfield was to her, her leaving it was painful. She said goodbye to Rachel as though she would never see her again. And Rachel, too, left in deepest dejection. Only Margaret, whispering and laughing with Rena, seemed glad to go, and jumped into the school bus, suitcase in hand, without even saying goodbye to Rachel.

CHAPTER SIXTEEN

Why have I blabb'd? Who shall be true to us
When we are so unsecret to ourselves?
SHAKESPEARE

IT was a golden October that year. A St Luke's summer. I
was now house captain, and enjoyed the responsibility. My
work was enthralling to me. I was discovering the delights
of Horace, and translating him into English verse for the
appreciative eye of Miss Burnett. I had also embarked on
the *Georgics* and was entirely (and for ever) charmed by
them, recognizing in them something of my own delight
in the cycle of the seasons. It seemed as I read them that I
looked out on Virgil's landscape from my windows. My
parody-making was put aside permanently. I was now on
the side of the angels. Bisto was gone, and of Margaret I saw
nothing.

My position threw me more than ever into the company
of my housemistress, Georgie Murrill. There were long
pleasant evenings spent in her room, and it was to her,
on one expansive occasion, that I spoke of the Chinese
garden.

'I was looking for you everywhere this afternoon,' said
Georgie, 'to talk to you about the house team. I felt we
ought to draw it up or they won't have sufficient time to
practise. You weren't playing games, were you? You were
crossed off the list. Where had you got to? Up the centre
path?'

'No, I didn't play games,' said Rachel. 'I was reading Byron.'

The white, gilt Adam fireplace was stacked with logs and the lights were turned out except for a reading lamp. Rachel sat opposite Georgie, her legs stretched out to the blaze, drinking coffee. To talk of teams bored her. She wanted to talk about herself. Now Bisto was gone, and Margaret inaccessible, she relied more and more on Georgie's company. The two became intimate. Georgie treated her as a privileged friend and discussed with her her private affairs. In this dangerous game, there were no known rules. Georgie allowed herself to invest Rachel with the discrimination and experience of an adult, while Rachel accorded to her the honest and faithful dealing of a contemporary. Younger than most of the staff, Georgie found in Rachel a touchstone which renewed in herself the qualities she had not quite lost, the curiosity, the ardour and the unexpectedness of youth. The poetry and music which were Rachel's passions, restored in Georgie pleasure in things which after years of teaching she had half forgotten. She reread Keats in order that she could understand Rachel's eager discussion of his poetry and his letters. She played Beethoven and Mozart duets with her and learnt the accompaniments of Schubert songs in order that Rachel could sing them.

'Don't let's talk about hockey teams,' said Rachel lazily. 'Let's play the "Jupiter".'

'It's too late. We should get into trouble.' (Thus were they subtly drawn into alliance against Bampfield.)

'Just the slow movement,' said Rachel, putting down her coffee cup, and moving towards the piano. 'Just the slow movement, played softly.'

But Georgie was irritated. She had wanted Rachel that

afternoon, and had not been able to find her. Possessive, she did not like to feel that Rachel was playing a game of which she knew nothing.

'You weren't in the prefects' room, or the library. Where *were* you?'

'Oh, I have my secret hide-outs,' said Rachel, with arrogant indifference.

There was a moment's silence. The firelight played on their faces and neither understood the other's expression, and it was now that Rachel, always a bad judge of the moment, chose to entrust to Georgie the one secret she should never have given up.

'As a matter of fact I *was* out,' she said.

Instinct told Georgie to make no comment. She sensed a coming confidence and waited for it.

'You know the shrubbery near the stables,' said Rachel slowly. Even as she spoke she was aware of an acute pain, like the extraction of a tooth. But it was too late to go back now. The roots were shifting. They would never take hold again.

'Yes.'

'There's a garden in there. A Chinese garden.'

'What do you mean exactly?'

'There are lakes, and it was once laid out as a Chinese garden, like a willow-pattern plate, with a pagoda and bridges and a boat and everything.'

'How did you get in? It's always been kept securely locked. Chief has never let anyone in there, because the bridges were so rotten. We explored it when we first came here from Somerset, and it's been locked ever since for safety.'

'Yes, the bridges *are* rotten.'

Into Rachel's mind came a picture of the scene. Almost she could visualize round it the blue rim of a plate.

'Go on, Rachel. Do tell me more. How did you get in?'

Rachel was silent.

'Do tell me.'

'I ... oh, well, I just go in there and read poetry,' said Rachel lamely, evading the question.

'In the middle of October?'

'Yes. It's warm in the boat. There are dried ferns and moss.'

'It sounds very romantic. You must take me to see it.'

'Oh, I don't think you'd want to go,' said Rachel quickly. 'It would mean scrambling through the fence and undergrowth, and...'

'You climb through the fence, do you?' asked Georgie, with amusement. 'How resourceful. Does anyone else know of this?'

'No,' answered Rachel. 'No. Nobody else knows about it.'

'Well, you know I shall keep it dark.'

'Please, Georgie, yes. You will, won't you?'

It was the first time that Rachel had used her nickname, and Georgie was touched and flattered. She did not understand the depth or the nature of the emotion that prompted it.

'Of course, I'll keep it quite secret,' she said. 'Cross my heart. It's time you went to bed.'

Rachel looked at her uncertainly. 'Is it a promise?' she asked.

The air was full of unacknowledged and unrecognized emotions.

'A sacred promise,' said Georgie, and Rachel left the firelit room for the dark gallery.

She walked slowly to the balustrade and looked down. The stairs were faintly visible in the distant light of a bulb burning in the hall. A smell of wood-smoke still hung about her clothes and its natural, associated smell, uncovering memories of leaf mould and wet branches, sent a slow thrusting pain into her heart. The garden was no longer her own. It had, in a sense, never been wholly hers, since Margaret and Rena used it – Rena? Yes, of course, she suddenly realized, Rena must know it, too. But their knowledge was as secret as her own, and a bond between themselves and the garden, even if of a different nature from her bond with it. And now she had voluntarily let a stranger in.

CHAPTER SEVENTEEN

A man betrayed is a man destroyed.
JOSEPH CONRAD

THE cataclysm broke about a fortnight later. The prefects were summoned by Chief. She was very pale, her eyes hard and piercing. She told us that Margaret and Rena had been discovered in some situation with which, it appeared, we were expected to be familiar, since it was not explained to us. The two girls were to be removed from the school. Pending the arrival of the parents, they were isolated in the infirmary, in separate rooms. They were, I learned afterwards, locked in. This nameless vice of which they were guilty was, apparently, infectious. We were told that as prefects we had a grave responsibility. It was up to us to keep our eyes open to see if the disease was spreading. We were adjured, like the apostles, to watch and pray.

Stunned, we prefects left the presence and retreated in conclave to our room. There I suppose we talked it over. We must have been like a group of savages holding a conference over their first sight of an aeroplane, and suffered from a similar, stultifying lack of vocabulary. How much the others subsequently found out, I never discovered. I myself applied for information to Georgie Murrill. After a little hesitation, and in a manner withdrawn and uneasy, she told me that the two girls had been found naked in bed together. This was quite sufficient for me. Though still ignorant of the exact nature of the vice, my fairly extensive reading had taught me that more than one person to a bed generally spelt wickedness. It was not, however, till that evening that it spelt anything more for me.

After supper I went to work in my study, a small room rather isolated in a distant wing of the house. I could hear a terrible crying and lamenting coming from the windows of the infirmary over which my study looked. I have never in my life heard such another sound. It was like the cries of the damned in hell. It went on and on interminably. The air was rent with grief. I left my work, profoundly moved, and went down to the prefects' room to sit in silence with the others round a dying fire.

*　　*　　*

Next day Margaret and Rena were taken away, and in the late afternoon Chief sent for Rachel. She was sitting in her small dark office, her back to the window, so that the girl's face was well lighted, but Chief's was blank with shadows. Chief knew something of the technique of interrogation. Without any preliminary, she asked Rachel whether she had ever spoken to Margaret about a book called *The Well of Loneliness*. She would accept no explanations. The answer must be yes or no. Yes, Rachel replied, they had had a conversation about this book which she had not herself read. Chief asked her if she knew what the book was about. Rachel found this difficult to answer. Dimly she was beginning to understand the nature of the crime committed by these two girls, but she was far from being able to put it into words. Chief accepted her assurance that she had not read the book, and told her that it was 'filthy'.

'This book has been brought into the school by Margaret,'

she went on. 'It has been found among her belongings. Even if you have not read it, and I accept your word over that, I find it difficult to understand why, as a prefect, you kept silent about it. You knew that Margaret had no right to have in her possession a book that had not been passed by her housemistress. You knew – you must have known – it had not and would never have been passed.'

Yes, Rachel knew it well enough. It was a breach of her prefectorial trust and she could do nothing but admit it.

'You are making it difficult for me to trust you,' said Chief. 'Other matters have now come to my knowledge that make it more difficult still. I am going to tell you exactly what they are, and I am going to ask you a question – a serious question – which I will give you time to think over before you answer.'

Chief then informed Rachel that it was *her* name to which Margaret and Rena had constantly referred. Rachel, it appeared, was the only human and decent individual at Bampfield. Margaret had stressed her unconventionality and her comfortable disregard for rules, and declared that her friendship with Rachel had alone made life in this prison tolerable. She admired Rachel for having the courage to criticize a hateful and tyrannical regime. With a legacy of parody behind her, Rachel could hardly deny that she had criticized it. Chief remembered that she had parodied a religious poem on one occasion, and that she never went to Communion. She mentioned these points, and Rachel felt that she was forejudged.

'How do I know that I can trust you?' repeated Chief, in a level, unemotional voice.

'I *haven't* read the book,' reiterated Rachel, clinging desperately to this one solid piece of evidence.

'I accept that. But you have talked of it.'

'Margaret talked to *me* about it.'

'What did she say?'

'I ... can't remember.'

'Perhaps she was speaking of it that night you met her in the back corridor.'

Rachel could say nothing. For a moment she was too stunned to recall the occasion.

'Have you forgotten?' persisted Chief. 'Some time ago ... in the spring term. You asked my permission to go round the house once. That was at ten o'clock. You abused that permission. At eleven thirty you were found standing in the corridor talking to Margaret.'

Rachel said nothing. Miss Burnett, for whom she had translated Virgil, and with whom she had enjoyed some of the keenest pleasure of her Bampfield life – Miss Burnett had betrayed her, had used her knowledge in an adult game of which Rachel knew too little.

Chief pressed home her advantage. How close was this friendship with Margaret, she asked, and when Rachel still could not trust herself to answer – and, in any case, what could she know of the degrees of friendship? – Chief leaned back in her chair and said with deliberation:

'It is difficult for me to believe that the friendship was not ... very close, that this was the *only* occasion on which you met Margaret at night.'

She waited for a moment for the words to take effect, and then leaned forward again to deliver another blow.

'You have found a garden, I understand – a Chinese garden in the far shrubbery. It is a place that I put out of bounds when we first came here. Yet it appears that you have been visiting it – by your own admission. Is it news to you that it was there that Margaret and Rena often met to carry on their filthy practices?'

The question hardly touched Rachel's consciousness. At the door of her mind hammered a far more monstrous question. How did Chief know that she had visited the garden? Her conversation with Georgie Murrill assumed a fearful personality of its own, pushed aside the lamenting of the two girls and the petty evidence of a book and a meeting by night. It stood, Judas-like, awaiting recognition. With a desperate effort, Rachel held the door of her thoughts against its insistent knocking.

Chief delivered her peroration: repeatedly, in her distress, Margaret had called the name of Rachel Curgenven. She had asked to see her, over and over again. Rachel Curgenven would have understood, she insisted in the hearing of her parents and of Rena's. She put it more positively. Rachel Curgenven *did* understand. Naturally, the parents demanded an inquiry. Their daughters had been corrupted. There was talk of a legal action against the school. Rachel would be called into court.

I am afraid of many things, of the dark, of heights, of a crowd, but no fear I have ever felt quite matches the inexorable terror of that phrase 'called into court'. This was not the splendid, purgative fear of the Chinese garden at night. This was the unholy, the unclean fear of the unknown hand in the dark, that cannot be parried.

Chief asked Rachel for a truthful answer to the accusation that she had both condoned and encouraged the activities of Margaret and Rena. She gave her three days to think it over.

Fear reigned at the centre of Bampfield, yet Rachel hardly

realized that this was so. Her own fear at those terrible words 'called into court' temporarily anaesthetized her against other, more dreadful certainties. She was absorbed with the problem of her own innocence. She did not visualize herself as the lynch-pin on which depended the future of a whole community. Still less did she foresee the fearful likelihood that if her guilt could be proved, the whole weight of the collective guilt of Bampfield could be shifted on to her shoulders. As yet, she was not isolated. She was still a part of Bampfield, and felt her fear and her own innocence, as a thread in the whole fabric. Despite Chief's interrogation, she did not feel that Bampfield, in the person of Chief, or Georgie, or Miss Burnett, had finally betrayed and jettisoned her.

It was to Georgie Murrill that Rachel turned, deeply distressed by her own ignorance and by her fears for her innocence, and still unable to believe that the final betrayal could come from her hand.

The forbidding label *Engaged* was hanging on her door, an injunction which Rachel had never dared to disregard before. But tonight she ignored it. She knocked firmly and went in without waiting to be answered. Georgie was sitting by her fire, reading, in her dressing-gown. She got up as Rachel came in, her face angry, her eyes defensive.

'There's an *Engaged* notice on my door,' she said.

'I know, I know, but I had to come. I've been with Chief.'

'I ... yes, I know you have,' answered Georgie.

Rachel suddenly realized the implication of her own words. She had, in fact, believed that Georgie could *not* have known. The 'Engaged' notice was her evidence. With the directness of which children are still capable, she said

149

quickly, 'You knew I was seeing Chief tonight? Then why the "Engaged"? You must have known I should come to you afterwards.'

'Really, Rachel, I've a right to put it on my door if I want to. Please go to bed. You'll feel better in the morning.'

'I can't go to bed. I want to talk to you.'

'It won't help to talk about it. There is nothing to say.'

'There is. There is.' Rachel was speaking with extreme difficulty. But the habit of self-control which Bampfield had given her stood her in good stead now. Her muscles taut, she was able to maintain an expression almost of indifference. Only her words had difficulty forcing their way out of her rigid mouth.

'I had to come and ask you ...'

'Look here,' interrupted Georgie, with a voice which shook with what Rachel thought to be anger. 'Listen. You lied to me. You come to me now because you are frightened, because Chief has frightened you. Did you tell her, as you told me the other day, that no one else knew about the Chinese garden?'

'I couldn't betray Margaret.'

'In other words, you lied to me?'

'No, no. I didn't lie. Not exactly.'

Rachel sat down uninvited and put her head in her hands. Georgie stood up and moved away from her, out of range of the firelight.

'I don't understand,' said Rachel. 'Why don't you explain to me? They must have felt love for each other, surely?'

At the moment, it was this that hammered at her mind, far more than her own predicament. 'They *must* have loved each other. Couldn't they have been forgiven? Why was it such a crime?'

'It was nothing but nasty experimentalism,' said Georgie.

'You didn't hear them –' Rachel went on – 'crying in the infirmary. It was a terrible sound. They must have loved one another to cry like that. What will they do now?'

'I don't know,' said Georgie. 'I am surprised you should be thinking about them. I hope you won't try to communicate with them. Your letters will be intercepted.'

'There's nothing to say. I don't want to write to Margaret. She probably hates me now.'

'Then you must have known,' said Georgie quickly.

'If I tell you I didn't, will you believe me?'

'I'd rather you thought it over before making such a statement.'

Self-control even of the Bampfield quality reaches its limit. Rachel could not go on. The gulf between their understandings was too vast. There was no means of bridging such a chasm.

'You'd better go,' said Georgie at last. She was sympathetic now, moved by Rachel's obvious distress. 'You'd better go. Think it over. Don't see me again until you've thought it over.'

And at the door of Rachel's mind still stood the Judas figure, whom she would not admit, whose features she could not bring herself to equate with Georgie Murrill's, who had promised to say nothing of the Chinese garden and had immediately betrayed the trust.

Next day, from her study window, Rachel looked down over the lime avenue to the stables, where she and Bisto had gone so often to feed Willy, and over the dark mass of the shrubbery in the heart of which lay the Chinese garden. She sat at her window most of that day. It was late in the afternoon when she saw three figures approach the bridge to the shrubbery and go over it to the locked gate. The unlocking of the gate gave them some trouble, it seemed. No doubt it was rusty after so many years of disuse. The garden and Rachel waited. One figure, that of Tarrant, pushed ahead. He was carrying something that looked like a bill-hook. The other two were Chief and Georgie Murrill.

In acute pain, Rachel saw their figures disappear under the dark leaves. Straining her eyes, she thought she could descry, every now and again, slight movements in the dark mat of branches and leaves. The ornamental ponds, though they could not actually be seen, were indicated by a small break in the density of the leaves and by lighter green of the trees and bushes that surrounded their moist shores, so there seemed to be two fairy circles on the dark carpet of the shrubbery. From the parapet outside her window where she was now leaning, Rachel thought she could see what she had never noticed before, a small pointed pinnacle, the top of the pagoda. They were there, walking round it, Chief prodding the soft wood, no doubt, with her shooting stick, Georgie looking with disgust at the boat in which she believed Rachel had witnessed and condoned, if not actually taken part in, perversities of whose nature she was even now largely ignorant. And Tarrant, what did he make of this expedition, of the dried fern in the boat, of the atmosphere of feverish curiosity and disgust?

It was almost dark now. The shadowy figures came out and locked the gate behind them. Next day, Rachel saw others, two of the estate men, and the boy with whom she had collected wood in the park, with barrows and tools. The garden was being destroyed.

Nature's polluted:
There's men in every secret corner of her
Doing damned wicked deeds.

Georgie Murrill's broken trust, monstrous though it was, could now at last be accepted in the light of this final, logical destruction of the garden – accepted as part of that adult world in which Rachel had never fully recognized that Georgie had her natural place. She could turn away from it now, almost with relief, to regard the problem of her own innocence. For she was not convinced that she was not guilty. She was assailed with a horrible doubt that she had in some way encouraged this nameless vice in Margaret and Rena by her own irreligious views and critical rebelliousness.

She could not trust her own armour against the forces which were moving in to the attack. Deeply soaked in the phraseology of the psalms, she sat alone in her study, her head in her hands, and repeated over and over again:

' "Deliver me from mine enemies, O God: defend me
from them that rise up against me.
O deliver me from the wicked doers: and save me
from the bloodthirsty men.
For lo, they lie waiting for my soul: the mighty
men are gathered against me, without any offence or
fault of me, O Lord.
They run and prepare themselves without my fault:
arise thou therefore to help me, and behold." '

The truth slowly began to clear. The bitter lamenting of Rena in the infirmary still haunted Rachel's ears. She had loved Margaret, and that love was nothing but a dirty device. Far more than technical innocence was involved. Primal innocence, the primal innocence of Traherne's orient and immortal wheat, was destroyed. What was whole had disintegrated. What had been perfect was irremediably stained. Rachel felt a bitterness against Margaret and Rena which strove within her against her sense of pity for their predicament. Her world had been a small one, but entire. If there was corruption, it had not appeared on the surface. If she could have advanced step by step into adulthood, her armour would have grown with her and protected her against later adversaries. But Bampfield was her armour and within it she lay naked like a white nut in its wooden shell. The walls of her fortress cracked, and in a moment she was beset.

Perhaps the bitterest thing of all was that no one came to her rescue. She was immediately cut off from her fellow prefects. She had no close friends among the girls. No one on the staff stood up in her defence. Her private coachings with Miss Naylor and Miss Burnett ceased, and she was told to work by herself for the time being. Even when she went out into the gardens, desperately tramping the lime avenues when the rest of the school was indoors, she was denied company, for the wood sheds were empty, and Punch looked away on the one occasion when she met her. She was hedged about with silence. Her study silence became a palpable oppression. She knew that she was left to prove her own innocence and felt betrayed by Bampfield itself, the setting of her misery and humiliation.

Death appeared as the one comprehending force, the one invariable and certain refuge. She realized, with awe, that he was always within call. Unable to reassemble from the ruins of her world a habitation in which to continue life, she decided to end it. She went about her business carefully. It was the third day of her agony and she was no longer enervated by doubt.

She needed a rope. Her trunk was kept in her study, and with a rug and a cushion it passed for a divan. Inside was a substantial piece of box cord. She locked the study door, took out the rope and made an efficient noose and slip-knot. Behind the door were three pegs and to one of these she fixed the rope. She had to tie it with the noose nearly touching the peg, for she was tall, and the hooks had not been designed for this purpose. She then removed her school tie and undid the collar of her blouse. She put a chair against the door, mounted it, and slipped her head through the noose. Fortified by the noble words of the Stoic wife: *Paete, non dolet* (Paetus, it doesn't hurt), she leaned forward a little and the noose tightened round her neck. Like a bather taking a plunge, she jumped forward and kicked over the chair. She found herself standing, with the noose drawn tight, but no more than mildly constricting her. The peg, after all, was not high enough to accommodate her.

CHAPTER EIGHTEEN

For being not mad, but sensible of grief,
My reasonable past produces reasons
How I may be deliver'd of these woes
And teaches me to kill or hang myself.
SHAKESPEARE

I WONDER now how it was that I recovered so quickly from this episode which brought me for a moment so close to death. For two days I had lived, virtually alone, while I searched myself to my depths to find the evil of which I was accused. The issue was one which must, I think, have driven me towards suicide in any case, but whereas, if I had indeed been guilty, I might well have made another and more successful attempt, I was now assured of my innocence; I felt the hands of Death himself had saved me, and some of the irony of that most ironic power entered into my soul, slipped easily like a lancet under my tortured skin, and relieved the agony.

I freed myself, untied the noose, and put it away in my trunk almost with affection. The absurdity, the scientific solecism, of having gone to all this trouble over slip-knots and pegs, without first finding out the drop necessary for my own height, struck me as exquisitely funny. I was keenly alive to the ludicrous. My own behaviour seemed as false and incongruous as Chief's sermons, and the impulse to destroy myself out of proportion to the circumstances, which were simply that an untrue accusation had been levelled against me. Truth was all that mattered. If Chief didn't believe me, was I to kill myself for it? The truth remained the truth, even if no one on earth believed it. I turned back to the psalms which had been my sole comfort during these desperate hours, and read:

O Lord, thou hast searched me out, and known me: thou knowest my down-sitting and mine up-rising; thou understandest my thoughts long before.

I copied it out very carefully and slowly in a commonplace book I kept at the time. Who it was that had searched me out and known me, I did not pause to consider. It could not have been God, since I did not believe in His existence. It may have been Truth, emerged from her well to spy out all my ways. When I had finished the reading and copying of this psalm, I went down to the prefects' room, and had tea with them in an embarrassed silence, broken only by orders to the fags, whose bright eyes darted from one to another of us solemn owls, and speculated no doubt on the responsibility which weighed upon our youthful shoulders. After tea, I took out the cards and suggested a game of bridge. The others were shocked at my frivolity and refused. I was relieved. I was only showing off, and what I really wanted was to have the cards to myself and play patience. I longed to have my mind made up for me, or at least confirmed in its secret decision, by the issue of a game. Should I go to Chief that night and take my stand on the truth, or not? I wanted the result of the cards (for my mind was in fact already made up) in order that I might regard it, if favourable, as a sign from heaven, or if unfavourable, as a challenge to my scepticism. So I played the games my father had taught me – *Les Huits* and *Senior Wrangler*. I really do not remember whether they came out or not. About an hour after tea, I rose and left the prefects sitting in a shy and dignified silence, not knowing what to think of me or what to say to me. I suppose they took it for granted that I was guilty of at least aiding and abetting Margaret and Rena in this nameless and abominable vice. I walked resolutely to Chief's study and told her in a few words that I was innocent. She believed me, without further question.

In Chief's silence – in the long silence which covered that episode during the remaining year I spent at Bampfield – I grew aware of the nature of the innocence which I had affirmed confidently that night, and which was accepted so readily. For me, at last, exposed and quivering, lay the lie which ran through the whole school like a nervous system. I was proclaimed innocent. I was once more part of the body of Bampfield, which like myself was declared innocent, uncorrupted. A diseased limb had been lopped off – as I should have been excised had I been found guilty – and the body was whole again. To myself, I was not innocent. I was corrupted with knowledge. Nothing I read, nothing I witnessed, nothing I experienced, would ever again have for me the radiance, the purity, the perfection which the Chinese garden had symbolized for me. The whole regime was based on a falsehood, in which I was ineluctably involved.

Years later, many years, in fact, since I had seen it on one of my periodic visits, I found myself travelling by car quite near Bampfield, now no longer a school. As I drove, first one and then another familiar name appeared on the sign posts, Long Clare, Clare St Thomas, Colverton, Stoke, and then, suddenly – Bampfield. An extraordinary sensation of weakness came over me. I slowed up, wondered, and then drove on. As I left the lane and its signpost behind me, all the pain of this symbolic rejection of the place, the overt acknowledgment that I would never again take the Bamp-field direction, pressed palpably against my throat so that I could hardly breathe. It was as if that power whom I had cheated there had thrust out his hand to remind me of his presence, in a rough, almost uncouth gesture, recalling our old acquaintance. I drove on, and slowly there was rebuilt in my mind the picture of the garden, that thought had lengthened in my heart. Bampfield had destroyed it with bill-hook and fire, yet Bampfield itself was now ashes to me, and the Chinese garden arose again, like a phoenix.

Beauty, truth, and rarity,
Grace in all simplicity,
Here enclosed in cinders lie.

AFTERWORD

The period between the 1928 obscenity trial of Radclyffe Hall's *The Well of Loneliness,* perhaps the most famous lesbian novel ever written, and the 1969 Stonewall Riots, the event commonly accepted as the originary moment of the international gay and lesbian liberation movement, might be called the Dark Ages of lesbian literature. The notoriety of the trial and the ensuing public outrage led to a powerful and pervasive backlash against any explicit form of lesbian self-expression in literature, art, and the media over the next four decades. Nonetheless, any number of significant lesbian fictions were published in Britain and the United States during these years, even if most of them were quickly consigned to the realm of obscurity. For many years, Rosemary Manning's *The Chinese Garden* has been known to lesbian scholars as one such work from this apparently dark period; yet even within this relatively small circle of critics, the novel was more *known about* than actually known. After its initial publication in 1962 by Jonathan Cape in Britain and Farrar, Straus and Giroux in the United States, the novel quietly went out of print—not, however, without gaining a few admirers, including the influential critic and author Anthony Burgess, a man not always kindly disposed to the lesbian novels and novelists of the 1960s. In 1984, *The Chinese Garden* made a brief reappearance, thanks to Brilliance Books, a small British gay and lesbian press; but despite this effort, the novel again vanished, ironically just before the first major wave of academic lesbian criticism and its reconstruction of the forgotten and obscured history of lesbian writing.

That the memory of Manning's novel stayed alive at all is thanks in great part to an entry in *The Lesbian in Literature,* a bibliography catalogued by Barbara Grier, the founder of Naiad Press, who earlier, under the pseudonym Gene Damon, was the book critic for *The Ladder,* the newsletter of the Daughters of Bilitis, the pioneering lesbian organization of the 1950s and 1960s.[1] Grier's compilation was a guide for stalwart lesbian readers in search of texts reflecting their lives and interests in a period when lesbians seemed, for all intents and purposes, invisible if not nonexistent. Tirelessly classifying any work that even remotely acknowledged female homoerotic desire, Grier ranked texts both qualitatively and quantitatively (through a code comprised of letters and asterisks) according to their respective degrees of lesbian representation. *The Chinese Garden* was listed as "A**," indicating "major Lesbian characters and/or action" with "very substantial quality of Lesbian material" (xix, xx). As such, it was deemed worth a potentially arduous search of libraries and used bookstores in order to find it.

For most of the novel's history such a search would have been necessary. In an ironic twist, *The Chinese Garden,* because it received little academic attention and was difficult to obtain, remained obscure and, as a consequence, went almost completely unremarked in the major works of lesbian criticism of the 1980s and 1990s. The one important exception is Terry Castle's *The Apparitional Lesbian.* In elucidating her theory that, historically, "ghosting" the lesbian object of desire (i.e., disembodying her or otherwise making her unreal) has been one of the few ways in which female homoeroticism could be represented without proscription, Castle glosses Manning's novel, among others, as a work in which "diligent ghost-hunters will find much to ponder" (59). Ghost-hunters may now rejoice.

With the publication of the Feminist Press edition, *The Chinese Garden* is available once more. But because the paradigms of what we expect from a lesbian text have changed so drastically in the four decades since the novel first appeared, to reintegrate it into the canon of lesbian literature—not to mention the canons of women's writing and twentieth-century British fiction—requires a bit of recontextualization. Manning's novel is permeated with "corruption" and "evil" in the setting of a sadomasochistic girls' school redolent—at times, literally—of decay and decadence. Nor is the book free from a certain level of melodramatic emotionality, which is hardly surprising in a narrative concerned primarily with the feelings and actions of adolescent girls in the throes of sexual awakening. Yet for many readers at the end of the century and the beginning of a new one, this does not present a very "affirming" or "positive" representation of lesbianism or nascent womanhood—which, understandably if sadly, has become the criterion by which many judge the intrinsic worth of any lesbian text.

Still, I would argue that *The Chinese Garden* is a valuable work, not merely for its artistic merit but also as a historical example of the state of lesbian and women's fiction in postwar Britain during a period of political and cultural transition, one that immediately preceded what has come to be known as the "Swinging Sixties." Accordingly, I would suggest that this novel should be considered within the various contexts it intersects: those of the literary tradition at large, of British women's writing, and of the literature of lesbianism.

The Chinese Garden is a powerful if often disturbing tale of forbidden desires between women and girls in a harsh and repressive homoerotic situation. The novel is set in the stultifying environment of an all-female boarding school run by an authoritarian and megalomaniacal headmistress and her staff during the 1920s. While the girls are forbidden any expression of love or sexuality between or among themselves, most of the staff, including Chief herself, are involved in a wide range of lesbian liaisons and intrigues. Accordingly, while homoerotic desire is pervasive, its very existence is unspeakable, and thus when Margaret, the school rebel, introduces a copy of *The Well of Loneliness* into this already unstable situation, it becomes the catalyst for a series of emotional and erotic explosions that threaten to undermine the hierarchies of authority upon which the school's philosophy—a curious one of making girls into "gentlemen"—is structured. In effect, to appropriate the Edenic metaphor Manning deploys throughout the narrative, Hall's novel becomes the forbidden fruit of the tree of sexual knowledge in a realm in which ignorance is, ironically, the order of the day. Rachel Curgenven, the protagonist and first-person narrator, finds herself caught in the middle of the crisis that follows, a not-so-innocent bystander who is reluctant to face the implications of her own desires. Torn among her dangerous attraction to Margaret, her infantile romantic friendship with the sentimental and childish Bisto, and her ambition to seek and maintain the admiration of the staff, Rachel is prematurely forced into a realization of the adult world that will mark the further course of her life.

In exploring such issues as adolescent (homo)sexual awakening, divided loyalties, personal integrity, and the struggle of the individual against the authoritarian regime, Manning presents a damning indictment of pedagogical corruption—a matter which held highly personal implications. For most of her life, Manning was a teacher and, ultimately, the head of a girls' school, all the while hiding her own lesbianism from all but the women with whom she formed relationships. Manning knew first hand not only the difficulties of maintaining a double life—the revelation of which could destroy her career—but also the pain of schoolgirl desire and betrayal. In *A Corridor of Mirrors* (1987), Manning's second autobiography, published a year before her death, the author at last shed light on certain unresolved mysteries in the novel, matters still unspeakable in the 1960s that can now be told. Rachel's story is, in fact, Manning's own, and through it she demands our reconsideration of the complex issues surrounding the sexual education of girls and those incidents between teachers and students that we now deem sexual harrassment.

The Chinese Garden as a Literary Novel

In "Pulp Politics" Yvonne C. Keller writes that two vastly different modes are discernible in lesbian fictions of the 1950s and early 1960s, namely pulp fictions and what she terms "literary lesbian novels" (18). The latter were those aimed for a "high-brow" (or even "middlebrow") audience and, as their designation implies, were written as *literature*, per se. *The Chinese Garden* goes to great lengths to establish itself as an unmistakably literary novel connected to a much larger and continuous cultural tradition, as if to establish its legitimacy and seriousness at a time when lesbianism was all too often regarded as the stuff that pulps are made of.

The epigraphs that begin the book and each of its chapters are culled from rather diverse sources (Virgil, Shakespeare, Traherne, Rilke, Lamb, and a few now-obscure Victorian poets), reflecting not only Manning's background as a classics mistress (which she ironically shares with her character Miss Burnett) but also the eclecticism of her personal tastes and influences. Like her protagonist Rachel, Manning as an adolescent sought solace and escape from an unhappy family situation through a consuming interest in the works of the Roman poets, and, in 1932, she earned a baccalaureate with second honors in classics from Royal Holloway College of the University of London.[2] But while Rachel imagines herself a latter-day Horace (or John Milton), she finds herself drawn into other myths and fictions deeply ingrained in the cultural imagination, even as these stories shape the plots that those around her seem determined to live out.

Milton sought in *Paradise Lost*, his epic retelling of the scriptural creation narrative, to "justify the ways of God to Man." But Rachel, despite her Miltonic aspirations, falls far short of comprehending the ways of women and girls—ways that culminate in a fall, not only for Margaret but, in a sense, for all concerned. In the Genesis account, sin, shame, knowledge (both carnal and other), and mortality enter the perfect prelapsarian world in the midst of the idyllic setting of a garden and through the combined agencies of a serpent and a woman. Except for a short-lived conversion experience, Rachel rejects traditional Judeo-Christian beliefs; perhaps, as a result, she fails to comprehend the erotic temptations, as well as the potential for sin and damnation, rife in the little Eden that Margaret has discovered, the secret hiding-place that Rachel subsequently usurps. Instead, oblivious to the literal and symbolic decay of the former pleasure grounds, she naively invests it with the exotic romanticism of the Chinese tale represented on the familiar Blue Willow tableware—that of the lovers who are metamorphosed into birds and escape the parents who forbid their love. The story, in its translation into Western culture, takes on the sentimentality of the Victorians who cherished the plates that memorialized it. Love conquers all, but only at a high price: the lovers are free, but lose their humanness and, by extension, their embodied sexuality. Ironically, events that occur in the Chinese garden will result in Margaret and Rena playing the roles of the forbidden lovers imprisoned by those who act in loco parentis; but there is no metamorphosis for the adolescent lesbians, only shame and ostracism. Not only are they cast out, but their Eden is destroyed by those playing the role of avenging gods.

Another "oriental" tale more deeply influences Rachel's romantic yet chaste fantasies about the garden: Samuel Taylor Coleridge's "Kubla Khan." Rachel, with "Coleridge's poems under her arm, and 'Xanadu' in her head," slips away to the garden to indulge her romantic adolescent imagination—a frame of mind conducive to the poet's fantastic images of an exotic and resplendent never-never land created and presided over by the legendary Mongol emperor (125). Almost comically, she sees herself as Kubla Khan and the decrepit garden her Xanadu, called into being, like the poem's "stately pleasure dome" (l. 2), by the decree of the poetic mind. Yet Rachel fails to understand the ramifications of the famous unfinished poem. As Paul Magnuson points out in *Coleridge's Nightmare Poetry*, things fall apart in Xanadu. The garden is not a natural one; rather, it reflects the order imposed on it by the artifice of the imagination that created it. Thus "the delightful dream is lost because order cannot be sustained" (Magnuson 39): for Coleridge "Alph, the sacred river" (l. 3) is an overwhelming force of nature, one that forces "a mighty fountain . . . / Amid whose swift half-intermitted burst / Huge fragments vaulted like rebounding hail, / Or chaffy grain beneath the thresher's flail" (ll. 19–22). Rachel trivializes Coleridge's river by associating it with the stream that feeds the stagnant pond; just as she, in her inexperience, does not differentiate between a placid stream and a chthonic, primordial energy, she cannot perceive the power of unsanctioned sexual desire to unsettle and shatter the carefully maintained order of Bampfield. Coleridge's poem runs its unresolved course in the song of an "Abyssinian maid" that reflects the poem's earlier reference to a "woman wailing for her demon lover," a phenomenon related by juxtaposition to the furious power of the river (ll. 39, 16). This wailing is eerily echoed when Rachel, late in novel, hears the cries of Margaret and Rena, each in solitary confinement awaiting her removal from the school, each wailing for her *demonized* lover (145). What Rachel fails to realize, as she reads Coleridge in the Chinese garden, is that just as "Kubla Khan" remains unfinished (the poet's reverie interrupted, or so he maintained, by the intrusion of the "person from Porlock"), so is her own self-absorbed dream world susceptible to the traumatic intrusion of the "real world."

Disruption, foreshadowing the crisis to come, appears in the person of Margaret, who intrudes upon Rachel's reading of Coleridge's other famous unfinished poem, "Christabel." This lengthy, quasi-Gothic verse narrative presents, in a highly fanciful medieval setting, the tale of Christabel, the only daughter of the widowed baron Sir Leoline. In the dead of night, Christabel discovers Geraldine, a damsel-in-distress, moaning in affliction outside her father's castle. Rescuing the girl, who is obviously of noble mien and who claims to be the victim of an abduction, Christabel furtively brings Geraldine into her own room and invites her to share her bed. Many hints are given in the poem to suggest that Geraldine is a lamia, a demonic vampire-like serpent-woman. The two sleep in each other's arms, and when they awake the next morning, Christabel is wracked with guilt and anxiety: "'Sure I have sinned!'" she exclaims (l. 381); yet her sin is never actually made explicit. The two young women approach Sir Leoline, but Christabel, whose powers of speech have been curbed by the "spell" Geraldine has cast on her, can only hiss, snakelike, and stumble as her father embraces her erstwhile tempter. The poem devolves into nonconclusion as Christabel, now herself the damsel-in-distress, embarrasses her father with the seemingly inhospitable plea that he "this woman send away!' (l. 627).

Margaret, significantly, reveals herself to Rachel just as the latter reads the portion of the poem relating the prophetic dream—ultimately unheeded—of Bracy the Bard, in which a white dove is strangled by green snake. The symbolism of chastity ruined by temptation is obvious. Margaret's response to the poem is curious, both for what she does and does not understand: "It could have happened here, couldn't it? . . . I found a grass snake here in the autumn, just like the one in the poem. Why do they look so evil? They're beautiful, yet they're evil. . . . Rachel, tell me why the most beautiful things are often evil?'" (129). In *Surpassing the Love of Men* Lillian Faderman has written extensively on the manner in which lesbianism, particularly in nineteenth-century male-authored literature, was regarded as the ultimate conjunction of beauty and evil.[3] But Margaret, although the social microcosm she inhabits would hardly consider her so, is quite innocent of the world and its judgments. She is puzzled by the symbolic conflation of evil and beauty as it is ascribed to snakes. She accepts—but surely does not comprehend the reason—that snakes are deemed evil, even though she sees their beauty. And as she reveals in her abortive attempts to discuss either Rena or *The Well of Loneliness* with Rachel, while she experiences the beauty of loving a member of one's own sex, she also understands that society—for reasons she finds inexplicable—proscribes it as an unspeakable evil.

Alhough Coleridge's poems fade into dreamlike inconclusiveness, events in the novel come to a horrifying close. A cruel pattern is in place, not so much as the result of design on the part of any single character but rather as part of a larger pattern at work in the universe— one that many would call fate.

The idea that random and unreflecting acts and words result in the seemingly accidental convergence of unstoppable forces is a salient factor in the novels of Thomas Hardy, one of Manning's favorite novelists. Manning was born in Weymouth, a town that plays a significant role in a number of Hardy's works, and, like her literary predecessor, drew much inspiration from the rural landscape and geography of their native Wessex, the ancient British kingdom that comprised most of present-day southwestern England. Bampfield is located in Devon, and, as is so often the case in Hardy's novels, the inanimate features of its setting take on personified qualities. The various elements of the garden reflect Rachel's distress, as well as her inspiration, and they are ultimately destroyed by the school's administration because the garden itself is "tainted" and "evil" as a result of the "sins" that took place therein. Hardy's most significant influence on *The Chinese Garden*, however, resides in the daringness of its theme. Hardy went against the grain of Victorian propriety and reticence in his representation of sexual matters. *Tess of the D'Urbervilles* (1891) and *Jude the Obscure* (1895) inflamed public sentiment with their honest—and sympathetic—depictions of extramarital sex, illegitimate births, and marital infidelity.[4] While, by the early 1960s, lesbianism was increasingly present in British women's writing, it was generally obliquely presented and often unnamed. That Manning would write so pointedly about the social reaction against female same-sex love—and with direct allusion to Radclyffe Hall's then-notorious *The Well of Loneliness*—is evidence of a Hardy-like level of courage. Moreover, Manning published the novel under her own name when she was the head of her own school, a gesture that surely was not without calculated risks.[5]

The Chinese Garden in British Women's Writing

Born in 1911, Manning was a member of the generation of British women writers who came of age during the 1930s and reached the apex of their literary careers in the 1950s and 1960s. Her contemporaries included, among the more notable, Mary Renault, Rumer Godden, Barbara Comyns, Sybille Bedford, Pamela Hansford Johnson, Mary Lavin, Elizabeth Taylor, Barbara Pym, Olivia Manning, Penelope Mortimer, Muriel Spark, Doris Lessing, and Iris Murdoch. This group is in many ways a disparate one, yet one in which several common threads can be detected, particularly their attempts to articulate the occluded erotic desires of women and girls. Following the literary trail blazed by Virginia Woolf (and, to some extent, Elizabeth Bowen), these women faced the challenge of creating narratives of women's lives in a world in which the traditional courtship plot was no longer the ideal and possibly no longer viable. The paradigmatic plot that begins with a young woman "coming out" in society (not, emphatically, in the neologistic queer sense of the term), passes through a period of conflict while she chooses the most suitable suitor, and concludes with her marriage may have served the purposes of Jane Austen and her contemporaries well; it certainly continued to predominate throughout the Victorian era. But the combination of such factors as the rise of late-nineteenth- and early-twentieth-century British feminists and suffragists, fin-de-siècle decadence, and the advent of literary modernism—along with the various discontents of female writers and artists that Woolf articulated in *A Room of One's Own* (1929)—culminated in a need for new female-engendered plots.[6]

For Manning and the women of her generation, the need for a new story to replace the courtship plot was further complicated by the devastation of two world wars, which annihilated a considerable portion of two consecutive generations of men. The shortage of marriageable men led to plots focusing on the lives of spinsters and, with increasing frequency, female friendships inside and outside of communities of women. Social and emotional interaction between women, whether in life or in fiction, frequently opens the door to homoerotic desire, as Virginia Woolf was thoroughly aware. In a 1931 speech to a women's group, Woolf predicted that "in fifty years I shall be able to use all this very queer knowledge that [the imagination] is ready to bring me. But not now . . . because the conventions are still very strong" (xxxix). Surely the 1928 obscenity trial of Radclyffe Hall's *The Well of Loneliness*—the very book that causes so much trouble in *The Chinese Garden*—made clear to Woolf the consequences of any direct or compassionate fictional representation of lesbianism. Hall's emotive plea for a humane understanding of "inverts" (as medical sexologists then termed homosexuals) was met with hostility and sensational notoriety. British justice found *The Well of Loneliness* obscene and banned its sale in the United Kingdom, a ban that stayed in effect until 1949. Nor was legal prohibition the only form of censorship threatening Manning and her contemporaries; many mainstream publishers, fearing public outrage as much as prosecution, were hesitant to issue texts that addressed "forbidden" matters. Accordingly, for British women writers working in that fifty-year period that Woolf foresaw (the end of which would coincide, aptly, with the prime of such authors as Angela Carter, Fay Weldon, Beryl Bainbridge, and Jeanette Winterson), any attempt to situate female homoeroticism in their narratives was, at the very least, a formidable challenge.

The 1961 lifting of the ban on *Lady Chatterley's Lover* (1928), D. H. Lawrence's sexually explicit novel of an adulterous interclass affair, effectively marked the end of stringent literary censorship in Britain even when the law relented the conventions were, as Woolf foresaw, "still very strong." In "Notes from the Underground" Patricia Cramer observes that prior to the 1970s, the decade of fulminating women's and gay liberation, there were only "three characteristic endings" for homosexuals in fiction: "the ending in marriage and suppression of homosexual feelings . . . loneliness and ostracism . . . and suicide" (180). While Manning challenges these limitations in *The Chinese Garden*, the "three characteristic endings" nonetheless cast their shadows over the plot: In her overly ambitious and never-finished play, Rachel expresses her horror and disdain for the institutional confines of marriage, an idea Margaret echoes in their secretive talk in the chicken shed; yet Margaret and Rena are ultimately banished, and Rachel, "tainted" by their implications, experiences the isolation and ostracism and, as a result, attempts suicide.

As Manning and her contemporaries strove in the face of these challenges, each in her own way, to create new stories about women's lives and desires, they were also affected by the influence of a factor unknown, for the most part, to their predecessors. Although the psychoanalytic theories of Sigmund Freud had been familiar to the intelligentsia since the early decades of the twentieth century, it was not until the period following the Second World War that the British mainstream had assimilated basic Freudian concepts. For many, though certainly not all, of these authors, Freud's writings on female desire, particularly those on hysteria and lesbianism, were highly problematic. In *A Corridor of Mirrors* (1987), Manning records that she was "repelled by a theory that has become a psychological cliché: that neuroses and indeed character traits in general are rooted entirely in our infant life, in the treatment that we received from parents, siblings, nurses, teachers. I chose to ignore the partial truth of this, finding it repugnant to my pride" (3). Freud's female pre-Oedipal complex, while in many ways a more humane approach to female homosexuality than those maintained by the medical sexologists who preceded him, nonetheless presents lesbianism as a form of arrested development, one in which the female subject fails to make the necessary shift of love objects (i.e., from mother to father and, subsequently, male lover) in the transitions between childhood and adolescence. While some lesbians—and many feminist literary critics—have found this a useful paradigm for lesbianism, it has often provided the means by which to infantilize lesbians and to see them as lost, pathetic creatures perpetually in search of a mother-figure.[7]

Fear of infantilization combined with fear of social ostracism, then, is at the heart of many narratives authored by Manning's generation. A brief examination of several notable works produced within a few years of *The Chinese Garden* reveals some highly suggestive similarities. Muriel Spark's *The Prime of Miss Jean Brodie* (1961) relates the coming of age of a group of young women who, as students in an Edinburgh girls' school, come under the influence of a charming if irresponsible and megalomaniacal teacher. While the physically consummated relationships in the novel are all heterosexual, the underlying desires—indeed those that, in some cases, motivate heterosexual misadventures—are homoerotic in nature.[8] Rather than employing a traditional linear narrative, Spark relates the events through flashbacks (contrasting the characters' burgeoning womanhood with their prepubescent years under Miss Brodie's tutelage in the 1930s) and also through what might best be called "flashforwards," in which the "Brodie set," in early middle age at the beginning of the 1960s, continue to live in the shadow of the charismatic teacher, now long dead. The movement between past and present is also seen in *The Chinese Garden,* in which the omniscient third-person narrator who describes Rachel's schoolgirl activities shifts, often abruptly, even within the same paragraph, to the vastly more sophisticated, if pessimistic, first-person voice of Rachel as an adult. We are, in effect, presented with two Rachels, and the contrast is nothing less than a Blakean dichotomy of innocence and experience, as the experienced Rachel delineates (and, it would seem, attempts to explain to herself) how the events of one school year made her the person she has become.[9]

The concept of the divided self, which is apparent in this doubling of Rachel's character, had become almost a commonplace in women's literature, thanks to the writings of psychologist R. D. Laing, the influential Scottish psychiatrist who challenged, however inaccurately, many of the prevailing notions about the causes of schizophrenia. Nowhere is this so apparent as in Doris Lessing's *The Golden Notebook* (1962), in which the protagonist, seeking to gain control over her life, separates the various aspects of it into entries in a series of notebooks. Lessing's novel shares with *The Chinese Garden*—and with Manning's autobiography *A Time and a Time* (1971), also a product of this period—a narrative self-analysis that borders at times on ruthlessness. Four decades later, such tellings may strike readers as excessive and solipsistic; yet such ferocious attempts to achieve knowledge are a historically important phase in the quest Woolf had foreseen: that which would allow women to tell the truth about their bodies and their desires. *The Golden Notebook* is also a disturbingly homophobic book, one that fears lesbianism as the ultimate female failure, the result of women being continually disappointed by the selfish and privileged behavior of men. Yet, perhaps not surprisingly, there is also a homoerotic girls' school story lurking in the background, as the protagonist fears that her daughter, who prefers the atmosphere of her school and the company of her teachers and the other girls to life at home with her mother, will lose her adolescent "new sexuality" (467).

In some sense, literary explorations of the homoerotic desires of girls (who, according to many psychological authorities, were merely going through a phase of polymorphous perversity that they would inevitably outgrow) are far "safer" than explorations of the homoerotic desires of more mature women. Many, even now, would be reluctant to apply the dreaded "l-word" to the activities of girls undergoing the paroxysms of puberty—and, indeed, most female-authored fictions of the time, *The Chinese Garden* included, avoid the word as much as possible. The girl, however, is the mother to the woman, and, as if an analysis of adolescent female sexuality would provide the key to understanding that of the adult woman, plots involving the same-sex attractions, obsessions, fantasies, and desires of female adolescents seem to have become ubiquitous in women's writing by the beginning of the 1960s. In addition to those novels previously discussed, plots containing girls and young women experiencing same-sex erotic frissons (often in the context of a school or convent and often involving teachers or other older women as the subjects or objects of desire) can be found in Brigid Brophy's *The King of a Rainy Country* (1956) and *The Finishing Touch* (1963), Sybille Bedford's *A Favourite of the Gods* (1963) and *A Compass Error* (1968), Maureen Duffy's *That's How It Was* (1962), *The Microcosm* (1966), and *Love Child* (1971), Iris Murdoch's *An Unofficial Rose* (1962), Elizabeth Bowen's *The Little Girls* (1963) and *Eva Trout* (1968) , Rumer Godden's *In This House of Brede* (1969), Olivia Manning's *The Camperlea Girls* (1969), and Beryl Bainbridge's *Harriet Said...* (1972).

Within a decade or two, adult women's desires of almost every variety would be quite openly discussed in literature. But, even in the early 1960s, *some* conventions, to paraphrase Woolf, were still very strong.

The Chinese Garden in the Lesbian Literary Tradition

Manning's familiarity with her lesbian literary heritage is demonstrated through a number of well-deployed allusions within the text. Those to Radclyffe Hall's scandal-provoking *The Well of Loneliness* are evident. Others, recognizable only to the lesbian cognoscenti, might easily be lost on Manning's mainstream audience. The most significant of these are the references to Clemence Dane, the author of *Regiment of Women* (1917), and to *Mädchen in Uniform*, Leontine Sagan's 1931 German film based on Christa Winsloe's play *Ritter Nérestan*

(1930), which in turn served as the basis for Winsloe's novel *The Child Manuela* (1933).

Regiment of Women and *The Child Manuela* are landmark works in a major subgenre of lesbian literature, the homoerotic girls' school narrative.[10] Early in the novel we see a group of students in their evening recreation, "the younger children . . . huddled against their desks in the outer cold, reading dog-eared novels from the library—novels which told of midnight feasts, adorable games mistresses and unbelievable escapades out of school bounds" (20). The allusion (most likely to Angela Brazil's juvenile-oriented fictions) is ferociously ironic, juxtaposing the ideal with the girls' noxious reality in their spartan, unheated surroundings. Against such cheerful and innocuous fare, Dane and Winsloe posit a very different story, one that finds echoes in *The Chinese Garden*.

"'Shakespeare has no monopoly on blank verse,'" Chief tells Rachel, rather perversely adding, "'You know Clemence Dane's plays well enough, and that's blank verse of the first order'" (85). Present-day critics are unlikely to share this perception. That Chief assumes Rachel's familiarity with Dane's plays is, I believe, suggestive of a form of lesbian vernacular, even between teacher and student, that implies recognition without ever naming the shared—and taboo—inclination, what today might be called "gaydar." In such cases, when acknowledgment of one's sexuality is not possible, allusions to lesbian icons—and the reaction of the other party to them—has often served as a means of identifying kindred spirits. And "kindred spirits," as Castle has shown, were certainly of significance to Dane.[11]

Born Winifred Ashton, Dane was an actress, playwright, spiritualist, and, early in her life, a teacher in a girls' school. Regiment of Women, as Hamer has aptly observed, "is not a cheerful lesbian love story" (84). Rather, it is, in Dane's own words, the story of "the monstrous empire of a cruel woman," schoolmistress Clare Hartill (1). Despite her apparent sadism, Clare is worshipped by her students and by the young novice teacher Alwynne Durand. It is only when Clare humiliates an adoring, oversensitive student and consequently drives the

girl to suicide that Alwynne breaks free of the older woman's power—
and marries a man. Although there is much to suggest that Dane herself lived a relatively happy lesbian life with her long-time secretary,
some recent lesbian critics have found *Regiment of Women* a homophobic text, which, to readers some eighty years on, it might well seem.[12]
It was, nevertheless, "the first British novel . . . devoted wholly to [female
sexual] variance" (Foster 257), and thus influential in the development of lesbian literature.

Although Manning does not directly allude to *Regiment of Women*,
she makes a curious reference to Winsloe's work, the plot of which
is similar to that of Dane's. *The Child Manuela*, like its more familiar film version, represents the fateful love of a student for her
young teacher. Manuela von Meinhardis, the orphaned daughter of
a Prussian army officer, is dispatched by her guardians to the confines
of a severe, militaristic girls' school. Her sole source of solace is Fräulein
von Bernburg, the only humane teacher among the faculty. Following
a school play—Schiller's *Don Carlos,* in which Manuela plays the title
role in male drag—she openly avows her love for her teacher. This
act earns the opprobrium of the sadistic headmistress, who orders
Manuela expelled. As a result, Manuela kills herself. For *Mädchen in
Uniform,* however, Sagan filmed two endings: one that remained faithful to Winsloe's original, and an alternative denouement (historically
the more familiar one to British and American audiences) in which
a revolution of little girls (to appropriate the title of Blanche McCrary
Boyd's book) saves the day.[13] Manning's direct reference to, presumably, the film version is nonetheless a relatively ambiguous one.
Just before relating the details of Chief's self-styled church liturgy
(which concludes, bizarrely enough, with her quoting Queen
Elizabeth's speech from Dane's *Will Shakespeare),* the adult Rachel
reflects, "We were not, despite the military nature of some of the discipline, 'Mädchen in Uniform'" (101). The narrative goes on to
explain that Bampfield allowed "startling breaches of rule in the interests of individuals," and that "the ripe eccentricity of so many of those
in authority over us" contributed to a "curious mixture of freedom and

restraint" (101, 102). Still, it is perhaps a tribute to Margaret's tenacity that her fate is not Manuela's tragic one, for she is punished as cruelly as Winsloe's heroine is. Yet if what Manning had in mind in her comparison was the "happy ending" version of Sagan's film, then it is so much more the pity that the girls of Bampfield lacked the courage to rise in defiance of the hypocritical injustice and homophobia perpetrated by a group of adult women who feared exposure of their own lesbianism.

In such an atmosphere, *The Well of Loneliness* becomes a lighted match to the powder keg of covert homoerotic desires. It chronicles the vicissitudes of Stephen Gordon, the only child of a wealthy peer who, having read the works of such sexologists as Havelock Ellis and Richard Krafft-Ebing, accepts his masculine daughter as an "invert" and treats her as he would a son. But the humane Sir Philip dies, and Stephen, despite her wealth, finds no acceptance from her mother or from the heterosexual world at large. While well intended, the novel is overly long, melodramatic, and relentlessly lugubrious. Regardless of its aesthetic shortcomings, *The Well of Loneliness* became an inspiration for several generations of lesbians who saw their reflection nowhere else in literature.[14]

Hall's book was published when Manning, like Rachel, was a sixteen-year-old student. It was a cause célèbre from the outset, with the editor of the *Sunday Times* calling for its immediate suppression (in language that is ironically echoed in the reactions of Bampfield's staff): "I would rather give a healthy boy or a healthy girl a phial of prussic acid than this novel. Poison kills the body, but moral poison kills the soul" (as quoted in Baker 223). The ensuing obscenity trial and appeal continued the controversy through the summer and fall of 1928.[15] Reviews and reports were, for the most part, "politely" vague about the book's subject matter, yet it seems fairly apparent that Rachel, who is not as sophisticated as she supposes, reacts with what Eve Kosofsky Sedgwick calls the "privilege of unknowing" (23). When Margaret attempts to discuss press accounts of the book, Rachel falls back on the innocence that is in fact ignorance:

"I wondered then what all the fuss was about. It seemed an important book, but I could not see why. My technical knowledge of sex was too meagre to enable me to relate what little I knew to the reviewer's account of the novel" (96–97). Rachel subsequently falls back upon this ignorance in order to protect herself from the implicating knowledge of exactly what Margaret and Rena are up to—even though Margaret, who believes that Rachel alone among the Bampfield students will be sympathetic to her situation, makes several attempts to discuss the matter. But Rachel exists on the boundaries between childhood and adulthood, as shown in her triangulation with Margaret and Bisto at the outset of the novel. She deploys her boundary-crossings strategically—even if only subconsciously—and retreats into the safe if childish realm of feeding Willy, the "pet" rat, with the sentimental Bisto when Margaret's demands become too disturbing. Nor is Rachel's "unknowing" without purpose, for it effectively saves her from sharing the fate that befalls Margaret and Rena.

Aside from the disturbances that Hall's novel supposedly elicits at Bampfield, other provocative traces of *The Well of Loneliness* appear in *The Chinese Garden*. Early in the narrative, Rachel describes Margaret in a manner that recalls Stephen Gordon and, by extension, Radclyffe Hall herself: "[S]he did not look like a schoolgirl. She was tall and thin, with a lean, brown, saturnine face, hair cut as short as a boy's, and heavy, often furrowing brows over dark eyes. A passionate reader and an inspired talker, she lived a life balanced between bouts of taciturn isolation, buried in books, and extreme gregariousness" (22). When Chief is described later on, she seems merely an older version of the same (50–51).

Indeed, Chief would appear to be a character straight out of *The Well of Loneliness*. Her history in the V.A.D. (Volunteer Ambulance Drivers) during the First World War recalls that of Stephen Gordon and her colleagues, who felt that the war gave them the one opportunity in their lives to be part of a community of women like themselves. Nor were Chief and her associates without real-life counterparts. Barbara "Toupie" Lowther, the daughter of a peer and the inspiration for Hall's story "Miss Ogilvy Finds Herself," had organized a famous unit of women drivers.[16] The fact that this unit played an important role in *The Well of Loneliness* was much noted during the obscenity trial, and many "patriotic" Britons felt that the honor of these war heroines had been impugned by association with "prurience" in the novel. Consequently, Chief's honor—such as it is—is threatened as well.

It is easy for the Bampfield staff to blame *The Well of Loneliness* for the girls' "nameless vice," as it deflects their own culpability (150). Manning's narrative is littered with clues regarding the lesbian intrigues of the various teachers, and Rachel becomes an inadvertent voyeur in the affair of Chief and Miss Burnett, even if she once again fails—or refuses—to comprehend what she sees. The reactions of the various staff members, as well as Rachel's retreat into ignorance, are demonstrations of the narrative phenomenon known as lesbian panic. Elsewhere, I have defined lesbian panic as

> the disruptive action or reaction that occurs when a character . . . is either unable or unwilling to confront or reveal her own lesbianism or lesbian desire. Typically, a female character, fearing discovery of her covert or unarticulated lesbian desires . . . lashes out directly or indirectly at another woman, resulting in emotional or physical harm to herself or others. This destructive reaction may be as sensational as suicide or homicide, or as subtle and vague as a generalized neurasthenic malaise. In any instance, the character is led by her sense of panic to commit irrational or illogical acts that inevitably work to the disadvantage or harm of herself or others. (2–3)

Rachel's stance of ignorance—which surely contradicts her self-image of the budding intellectual—is, I would suggest, a mild form of lesbian panic. It stems from her own attraction to Margaret, a situation that is exacerbated not only by Rachel's guilt over the growing revulsion she feels towards Bisto's emotional demands but also by

Margaret's growing interest in the banal Rena and a confusing web of emotional attachments with various teachers. In effect, Rachel is pulled in all directions by a wide variety of homoaffectional—if not downright homoerotic—inducements. Her responses, then, are those of one caught in the crossfire and—given her youth and confusion— readily forgivable, for the main recipient of the resulting disadvantage or harm is really herself. It would be heroic if she were to rise to Margaret's defense, but, in practical terms, such heroism would also be utterly self- destructive and, furthermore, to no avail.

What is less forgivable, however, are the reactions of the staff. The extremes of severe discipline and utter laxness that shape the day-to- day life of Bampfield and the liaisons between the various mistress- es would make it seem as if the school does not really exist for the purpose of teaching young women so much as for the purpose of cre- ating an isolated lesbian microcosm in which Chief and her minions can pursue their amours without constraint. In light of the homophobia of society at large, the desire for such an separatist community is under- standable, yet it does not take into consideration how it affects the girls whom these women are training, however *queerly,* to be "perfect English gentlemen." While Bampfield may be an ideal lesbian train- ing ground, the dangers of detection, particularly in light of the cul- tural reaction against Hall and her book and the stereotype of homosexuals as pederasts, make *overt* lesbianism the absolute taboo— indeed, so taboo that their "vice" must remain unnamed.

The discovery of Margaret and Rena naked in bed together makes that which was hidden all too obvious and, accordingly, all traces must be erased—including the garden, which is, as in scripture, the site of the original sin. The expulsion and destruction that ensue in the scrip- tural account are replicated in the vengeance demanded by the "Gud" whom Chief has created in her own image and likeness.

The Chinese Garden as Autobiography

"To come out at the age of seventy . . . to come out of what, I ask myself?" (1). So Rosemary Manning began her second autobiography, *A Corridor of Mirrors*. To set the context for the events of her life, she begins by explaining her earlier reluctance to acknowledge her lesbianism:

> There was my upbringing in an overwhelmingly masculine family, and there was my career. Though lesbians suffered no legal penalties [in Britain] as male homosexuals did, there was a strong prejudice against them . . . and an active unwritten law against their holding posts which brought them into contact with children and young people: it was generally believed (and this is so today) that most gay people are pederasts. (1)

Because Manning was a teacher and, eventually, the headmistress of a school, her apprehensions are quite understandable. They are also the foundation for much of what is said—and not said—in *The Chinese Garden*.

Manning's father was a respected physician, her mother a former nurse, "a late-nineteenth-century career woman" *(Corridor of Mirrors* 10). The Mannings had three sons early in their marriage; in 1911, when May Manning was forty-four, she gave birth to her only daughter. The early influences on Manning's life were the masculine activities of her father and brothers. Eventually, she was sent to a boarding school for girls in Devon, a school that served as the model for Bampfield, where she stayed for six years. While she was at school, her parents' marriage disintegrated, and her father eventually abandoned his family to live, quite openly, with his mistress, a woman of mixed race. To escape the emotional and social ramifications of what amounted to nothing less than a scandal in late 1920s Britain—and to escape the trauma of her mother's hysterical responses to the situation—Manning turned to her studies. Indeed, as her earlier biography *A Time and a Time* indicates, she was a lifelong student of literature and the humanities, often to the detriment or exclusion of personal relationships.

Manning nevertheless persisted in a series of abortive affairs, at first with men and women alike, but later with women only. A truly painful text to read, *A Time and a Time* reveals, perhaps unselfconsciously, the chronic depression that leads Manning not only to two suicide attempts but also to the almost willful destruction of her relationships and virtually any situation that offered the promise of happiness.[17] In spite of her personal unhappiness and her apparent inclination to ruthless self-dissection, Manning was able to successfully maintain a career in education while producing several novels and numerous children's books and becoming, in her own words, a "middle-class intellectual" *(Corridor of Mirrors* 186).[18] Manning's life did not end tragically, however; she was, in a sense, someone who had spent a lifetime waiting for both women's and gay liberation to happen. In her sixties and seventies, she became increasingly outspoken on social issues and, as *A Corridor of Mirrors* demonstrates, a rational and eloquent survivor of decades of oppression and repression. She died quietly in 1988, at the age of seventy-six.

A Corridor of Mirrors fills in a variety of gaps, not only those quite purposefully left out of her personal history in *A Time and a Time* but also a very crucial lacuna in *The Chinese Garden.* Of the novel she writes: "It was autobiographical, the most truthful book I have ever written about myself" (55). As previously discussed, Rachel remains strangely, almost unrealistically ignorant of sex and sexuality even after Margaret and Rena are caught in the act. While her feelings of betrayal over Georgie Murrill's revelations to Chief are understandable from an adolescent point of view, the teacher's actions seem reasonable enough, as Manning, herself as an educator (and, by extension, her adult narrator) would realize. Late in life, she finally felt free to reveal the true nature of Georgie's betrayal, which was, perhaps not surprisingly, the ultimate crime of which lesbian educators are all too frequently—and often all too falsely—accused:

> When I was sixteen I fell deeply in love with my housemistress, whom I call Georgie Murrill. Chief herself was a lesbian and was having affairs with several members of the staff,

some concurrently. Those she cast off stayed on, a little army of devotees. Georgie Murrill was one of them. It was my misfortune that I should have felt for her far more than the usual schoolgirl 'crush'. . . . It was unfortunate for me for two reasons: firstly because [her] mind was trivial and narrow. . . . Secondly, and far more importantly, she exploited me sexually. . . . I was woefully ignorant about sex and certainly far from being aware of my lesbian leanings. She subscribed to the general double standards of Bampfield whereby the pretence was kept up that every member of the staff was 'normal'. . . . Georgie Murrill did boast of having a young man. At one moment she was pulling me into bed with her, and the next she was extolling the pleasures of her affair with Chief's red-headed nephew. . . . She was in fact using me to provide her with some of the sexual excitement she lost when Chief jettisoned her. Physically, . . . we did not get much further than cuddling and petting . . . but this aroused feelings I could not fully understand. It would have been better if she had gone the whole way and given me some experience of sex as enjoyable and productive of happiness, instead of behaving in a way that left me still ignorant, frightened of my overwhelming sensations, and burdened with inhibitions and fears which were to last me half a lifetime.

My affair with Georgie Murrill was very damaging and I have no forgiveness for her whatever. For this essentially untrustworthy, mean little personality I reserved one of the only bitter remarks in the novel: 'Her cowardly desire to appear on the side of the angels led her to jettison the child she should have protected. I think it is for the Georgie Murrills of this world that the millstones have been reserved [63].' *(Corridor of Mirrors* 62–63)

The "millstones" allude to the words to the oft-quoted scriptural injunction about exposing children to scandal: "But whoso shall offend one of these little ones . . . it were better for him that a millstone were hanged about his neck, and that he were drowned in depth of the sea" (Matthew 18.6). For Manning, though, the scandal of Georgie Murrill's conduct is not so much the sexual relationship between teacher and student as it is her deceptiveness and hypocrisy. The offense does not reside in the sexual act itself but rather in the lies and the shame that surround it, lies and shame that leave lasting scars.

Some will, no doubt, take exception to Manning's assertion that an honest and sexually fulfilling relationship between a teacher and student might be possible, not to mention useful. But that is beside the point. What is important to realize, if we are to understand the implicit message of *The Chinese Garden* at all, is that the evil and corruption that infiltrate Bampfield do not reside in the love between Margaret and Rena, in Rachel's feelings for Georgie or any other member of the staff, or in the influence of books such as *The Well of Loneliness*. Nor, for that matter, do they reside in the amours of Chief and her minions in and of themselves, but instead in the hypocrisy of those who deem love and desire between women evil and unnatural, even while they themselves engage in it, and who would inflict their own shame on others, the shame of what we have come to call the closet. It is a lesson which, some four decades after *The Chinese Garden* was first published, many have yet to digest.

Patricia Juliana Smith
Los Angeles, California
August 1999

Notes

1. Because her reviews began in 1966, four years after the novel's publication, Grier did not review *The Chinese Garden* for *The Ladder*. (The reviews are collected in one volume as *Lesbiana: Book Reviews from the Ladder*.) She did, however, review Manning's first autobiography, *A Time and a Time* (see n. 17). Inexplicably, *The Chinese Garden* is not mentioned in *Sex Variant Women in Literature*, the redoubtable bibliographical reference authored by Jeannette H. Foster, Grier's mentor.

2. For a detailed narrative of the familial disruptions of Manning's adolescence, see *A Corridor of Mirrors* (64–91). I would suggest that the name of the mysterious and seemingly decadent classics mistress in *The Chinese Garden* may well be an allusion to Ivy Compton-Burnett (1884–1969), the lesbian author of a number of tartly satiric novels of manners who had herself earned a baccalaureate in classics from Royal Holloway in 1906, a quarter of a century before Manning.

3. See Faderman (277–94). See also Bram Dijkstra on "decadent" lesbianism (152–59) and lamias and snake women (305–14) in fin-de-siècle art.

4. Hardy was, moreover, responsible for one of the most curious representations of female homoeroticism in Victorian literature. In his *Desperate Remedies* (1871), an older woman lures her young maid into her bed, where she proceeds to kiss her and interrogate her as to whether she has ever been kissed by a man. This lengthy scene, although it precedes Freudian psychoanalytical theory by several decades, nonetheless contains numerous elements of Freud's concepts of lesbianism in particular and homosexuality in general, especially in its conflation of erotic and maternal desires, and in the oddity of the two women sharing the uncommon name Cytherea, an appellation of the goddess Venus. See Foster (93) and Faderman (172).

5. In *A Corridor of Mirrors*, Manning writes that prior to her "coming out" in a television interview in 1980, "I had kept my lesbianism a secret all my life. I had not even spoken of it to more than one or two close friends, though it must have been known to most of my circle" (1). This statement,

I believe, is somewhat disingenuous. In 1965, Manning reviewed for *Arena Three* Frank Marcus's play *The Killing of Sister George*, which depicts the fall of a butch lesbian television actress as she is written out of her role in a popular soap opera. The magazine was produced by the Minorities Research Group (MRG), which, according to Emily Hamer, was "the first explicitly and dedicatedly lesbian social and political organization in Britain. The importance of the Minorities Research Group and its magazine *Arena Three* cannot be overstated. Even lesbians who did not support the MRG were affected by its existence—shades of *The Well of Loneliness*" (166). Hamer reports that in her review, "Manning could not get over the fact that [the play] was being performed, let alone to acclaim, given its subject-matter" (170). This would suggest that Manning was somewhat more open about her lesbianism—and that her "circle" was rather larger—than she maintains in her autobiography.

6. This overview of the evolution of female-authored plots is, of necessity, a very simplified one. For one of the best extensive studies of what amounts to a paradigm shift in women's fictions, see Rachel Blau DuPlessis, *Writing Beyond the Ending*.

7. For the most pertinent aspects of Freud's theories as they apply here, see his essays "Female Sexuality" (*Complete Psychological Works* 21: 221–46), "Femininity" (22: 113–17), and "The Psychogenesis of a Case of Homosexuality in a Woman" (18: 145–72). I have stated elsewhere my feelings about the overuse by feminist critics of the pre-Oepidal complex as a means of understanding lesbianism; see Smith (202, n. 26).

8. For an analysis of the underlying homoerotic tensions in *The Prime of Miss Jean Brodie,* see Smith (84–92).

9. Indeed, Rachel (speaking as the adult third-person narrator) makes a rather curious allusion to William Blake's *Songs of Innocence and Experience* in the scene in which Rachel first discovers the garden: "She entered an exotic world where she breathed pure poetry. It had the symmetry of Blake's tiger" (78). Whether the ambiguously placed "it" refers to the "exotic world" or the "pure poetry" she breathes is beside the point. What is significant is that Rachel, at this point still in the throes of naivete, connects

the garden not with an image from Blake's "Songs of Innocence" but rather with "The Tyger," one of the "Songs of Experience." Because Rachel's perception is filtered through the experience of her adult narrative persona, it can be seen as an ironic foreshadowing of the sexual knowledge that will originate from this site.

10. On the lesbian girls' school novel, see Martha Vicinus (600–22) and Corinne E. Blackmer (32–39). See also Alison Hennegan (5–16) for a comparison of *The Chinese Garden* with homoerotic British boys' school fictions.

11. See Castle, *Noël Coward and Radclyffe Hall* (21–22, 99–101).

12. For various views on Dane and her novel, see Foster (257–60), Faderman (341–43), and Hamer (84–88).

13. On Winsloe's novel, see Foster (236–38); Foster first pointed out the parallels between *Regiment of Women* and *The Child Manuela* (259). Curiously, Louise, the tragic student in Dane's novel, like Manuela plays a male role (Prince Arthur in Shakespeare's *King John*) in an emotionally fraught school play. On the film *Mädchen in Uniform*, see Andrea Weiss (8–11).

14. On the extraordinary ongoing influence of *The Well of Loneliness* in lesbian culture, see Hamer (94–117).

15. The particulars of the trial are well documented and too complex to relate here. For detailed account of the controversy and trial, see Michael Baker (223–49) and Edward de Grazia (178–93).

16. On Lowther, her war service, and her friendship with Hall, see Hamer (50–53) and Baker (125–27). The friendship ultimately ended, a casualty, for various reasons, of the trial.

17. *A Time and a Time* was, for the early 1970s, a relatively frank lesbian autobiography. It was not, however, an unqualified success with lesbian audiences. Its relentlessly self-analytical and self-justifying tone, along with Manning's disdain for lesbian subculture, earned the book a scathing review from Barbara Grier in *The Ladder:* "[It] is boring, it is in bad taste, it isn't necessary. . . . [S]he goes through several women without much attempt to work out a relationship past the bedroom door. . . . I can't help wondering what would happen to her precarious balance (mentally) if some

friend simply pointed out to her the one glaring fact she has left out of her yawning autobiography, that she is self-centered to the point of having mental myopia" *(Lesbiana,* 282–83). While this review is needlessly ruthless—an attitude no doubt inspired by the extremes of the then-nascent lesbian identity politics that had little use for negativity or dissent within the ranks—Manning herself was eventually able to see the book's flaws. In *A Corridor of Mirrors* she writes that her life-long "inability to take myself quite seriously has remained, though you might hardly think so from reading this book. It disappoints me. . . . When I reread *A Time and a Time* recently, I thought it the funniest book I had ever written" (229). *A Corridor of Mirrors* is, by contrast, a compelling, unselfpitying, and often amusing chronicle of life as a British lesbian during the pre-liberation years.

18. Manning's other novels are *Remaining a Stranger* (1953), *A Change of Direction* (1955), *Look, Stranger* (1960), *Man on a Tower* (1965), and *Open the Door* (1983); the first two were published under the pseudonym "Mary Voyle." Her children's books include the Susan and R. Dragon series: *Green Smoke* (1957), *Dragon in Danger* (1959), *The Dragon's Quest* (1961), *Dragon in the Harbour* (1980); also *Arripay* (1963), *Boney Was a Warrior* (1966), *Heraldry* (1966), *The Rocking Horse* (1970), and *Railways and Railwaymen* (1977). Additionally, she edited medieval miracle plays, a selection of William Blake's poetry, and Charles Dickens's *Great Expectations* for juvenile readers.

Works Cited

Bainbridge, Beryl. *Harriet Said . . . .* London: Duckworth, 1972.

Baker, Michael. *Our Three Selves: The Life of Radclyffe Hall.* New York: Morrow, 1985.

Bedford, Sybille. *A Compass Error.* London: Collins, 1968.

———. *A Favourite of the Gods.* New York: Simon and Schuster, 1963.

Blackmer, Corinne E. "The Finishing Touch and the Traditions of Homoerotic Girls' School Fictions." *Review of Contemporary Fiction* 15, no. 3 (1995): 32–39.

Bowen, Elizabeth. *Eva Trout, or Changing Scenes.* New York: Knopf, 1968.

_____. *The Little Girls.* New York: Knopf, 1963.

Brophy, Brigid. *The King of a Rainy Country.* London: Secker & Warburg, 1956.

_____. *The Finishing Touch.* London: Secker & Warburg, 1963.

Castle, Terry. *The Apparitional Lesbian: Female Homosexuality and Modern Culture.* New York: Columbia University Press, 1993.

_____. *Noël Coward and Radclyffe Hall: Kindred Spirits.* New York: Columbia University Press, 1996.

Coleridge, Samuel Taylor. "Christabel." In *The Complete Poetical Works of Samuel Taylor Coleridge.* Ed. Ernest Hartley Coleridge. Vol. 1. Oxford: Clarendon, 1912. 213–36.

_____. "Kubla Khan." In *The Complete Poetical Works of Samuel Taylor Coleridge.* Ed. Ernest Hartley Coleridge. Vol. 1. Oxford: Clarendon, 1912. 295–98.

Cramer, Patricia. "Notes from Underground: Lesbian Ritual in the Writings of Virginia Woolf." In *Virginia Woolf Miscellanies: Proceedings of the First Annual Conference on Virginia Woolf.* Ed. Mark Hussey and Vara Neverow-Turk. New York: Pace University Press, 1992. 177–88.

Dane, Clemence. *Regiment of Women.* New York: Macmillan, 1917.

de Grazia, Edward. *Girls Lean Back Everywhere: The Law of Obscenity and the Assault on Genius.* New York: Vintage, 1993.

Dijkstra, Bram. *Idols of Perversity: Fantasies of Feminine Evil in Fin-de-Siècle Culture.* New York: Oxford University Press, 1986.

Duffy, Maureen: *Love Child.* New York: Knopf, 1971.

———. *The Microcosm.* London: Hutchinson, 1966.

———. *That's How It Was.* London: New Author's, 1962.

DuPlessis, Rachel Blau. *Writing Beyond the Ending: Narrative Strategies of Twentieth-Century Women Writers.* Bloomington: Indiana University Press, 1985.

Faderman, Lillian. *Surpassing the Love of Men: Romantic Friendship and Love between Women from the Renaissance to the Present.* New York: Morrow, 1981.

Foster, Jeannette H. *Sex Variant Women in Literature.* Tallahassee: Naiad Press, 1985.

Freud, Sigmund. *Standard Edition of the Complete Psychological Works.* Trans. and ed. James Strachey. 24 vols. London: Hogarth Press, 1953–74.

Godden, Rumer. *In This House of Brede.* New York: Viking, 1969.

Grier, Barbara. [Gene Damon, pseud.] *The Lesbian in Literature.* 3rd. ed. Tallahassee: Naiad Press, 1981.

———. *Lesbiana: Book Reviews from the Ladder.* Tallahassee: Naiad Press, 1976.

Hall, Radclyffe. *Miss Ogilvy Finds Herself.* London: Heinemann, 1934.

———. *The Well of Loneliness.* London: Jonathan Cape, 1928.

Hamer, Emily. *Britannia's Glory: A History of Twentieth-Century Lesbians.* London: Cassell, 1996.

Hardy, Thomas. *Desperate Remedies.* London: Tinsley, 1871.

Hennegan, Alison. Introduction to *The Chinese Garden.* By Rosemary Manning. London: Brilliance Books, 1984.

Keller, Yvonne C. "Pulp Politics: Strategies of Vision in Pro-Lesbian Pulp Novels, 1955–1965." In *The Queer Sixties.* Ed. Patricia Juliana Smith. New

York and London: Routledge, 1999. 1–25.

Lessing, Doris. *The Golden Notebook*. New York: Simon and Schuster, 1962.

Mädchen in Uniform. Dir. Leontine Sagan. Perf. Hertha Thiele and Dorothea Wieck. Deutsche Film-Gemeinschaft, 1931.

Magnuson, Paul. *Coleridge's Nightmare Poetry*. Charlottesville: University Press of Virginia, 1974.

Manning, Olivia. *The Camperlea Girls*. New York: Coward McCann, 1969.

Manning, Rosemary. *A Corridor of Mirrors*. London: Women's Press, 1987.

———. [Sarah Davys, pseud.] *A Time and a Time: An Autobiography*. London: Calder & Boyars, 1971.

Murdoch, Iris. *An Unofficial Rose*. New York: Viking, 1962.

Sedgwick, Eve Kosofsky. "Privilege of Unknowing." In *Tendencies*. Durham: Duke University Press, 1993. 23–51.

Smith, Patricia Juliana. *Lesbian Panic: Homoeroticism in Modern British Women's Fictions*. New York: Columbia University Press, 1997.

Spark, Muriel. *The Prime of Miss Jean Brodie*. New York: Dell, 1961.

Vicinus, Martha. "Distance and Desire: English Boarding School Friendship, 1870–1920." *Signs: Journal of Women in Culture and Society* 9, no. 4 (1984): 600–22.

Weiss, Andrea. *Vampires and Violets: Lesbians in Film*. Harmondsworth, England: Penguin, 1993.

Winsloe, Christa. *The Child Manuela*. Trans. Agnes N. Scott. New York: Farrar, 1933.

Woolf, Virginia. "Speech before the London/National Society for Women's Service, January 21, 1931." *The Pargiters: The Novel-Essay Portion of* The Years. Ed. Mitchell A. Leaska. New York: Harcourt, 1978. xxvii–xliv.